For the first time since she'd met him, the facade of perpetual ennui disappeared and she saw real emotion on his face.

His eyes darkened to the deep green of the sea in a storm and his lips parted in a smile that had nothing to do with mirth. Then he moved closer until she could swear she felt the heat of his body through the air between them. "Yes, Miss Prescott, after our wedding, I would have taken you to my bed. But a meeting of bodies is one thing and a meeting of minds is quite another. I had hoped that, after some time together, the latter would develop from the former."

"And I hoped quite the opposite," she said, surprised. "It cannot be possible to enjoy the marital act with a complete stranger."

In response, he laughed. And something deep inside her trembled in answer to the sound. "Would you care to wager on the fact?"

Author Note

When it came time to choose a setting for my current book, I found that I was not quite ready to move on from Comstock Manor, the childhood home of Faith, Hope and Charity Strickland in my Those Scandalous Stricklands series.

The Great Houses of Britain have always fascinated me, as does the way that a family can accumulate possessions and memories after living for generations in the same space. It has been fun for me to imagine the odds and ends that the Strickland family collected, and to create the rooms that housed them.

But by the end of the story, it surprised me how well I knew my way around a house that has never existed. When my characters walked from room to room, I always knew when they were turning left or right. When they used the passages between the walls, I knew how far they had to walk, and where they would come out.

If you read my other books, I hope that the manor house has become real to you as well, and that you enjoy exploring some new rooms.

CHRISTINE MERRILL

*The Brooding Duke
of Danforth*

Recycling programs
for this product may
not exist in your area.

ISBN-13: 978-1-335-63515-0

The Brooding Duke of Danforth

Copyright © 2019 by Christine Merrill

Printed in U.S.A.

www.Harlequin.com

Christine Merrill lives on a farm in Wisconsin with her husband, two sons and too many pets—all of whom would like her to get off the computer so they can check their email. She has worked by turns in theater costuming and as a librarian. Writing historical romance combines her love of good stories and fancy dress with her ability to stare out the window and make stuff up.

Books by Christine Merrill

Harlequin Historical

Wish Upon a Snowflake
"The Christmas Duchess"
The Secrets of Wiscombe Chase
The Wedding Game
The Brooding Duke of Danforth

Those Scandalous Stricklands

Regency Christmas Wishes
"Her Christmas Temptation"
A Kiss Away from Scandal
How Not to Marry an Earl

The Society of Wicked Gentlemen

A Convenient Bride for the Soldier

The de Bryun Sisters

The Truth About Lady Felkirk
A Ring from a Marquess

Visit the Author Profile page
at Harlequin.com for more titles.

To James. For knocking down doors.

Prologue

'Was there no other way than to spend an evening here?' Lady Beverly tapped her foot, fighting against the rhythm of the music. 'Meagre refreshments, tepid dancing and tiresome company will make for the dullest evening imaginable.'

'You did not have to accompany me, Lenore,' replied Benedict Moore, Fourth Duke of Danforth. 'But as you keep reminding me, it is time I married. One hunts for rabbits in the field and fish in the stream. When one is hunting for a wife, one comes to Almack's.'

'You are correct that I have been telling you so for years. But why have you suddenly decided to listen?'

'Considering the family history, I might not have much longer to make such a decision.' *Or the faculties to do so.* He did not add the comment, but remembering his father's final year, the possibility that he might end his days babbling in a sickbed was never far from his mind.

'You are of an entirely different sort than your father,' Lenore said. 'You are not given to excesses of diet or temper. If anything, Danforth, people say that you are not emotional enough. I doubt you will be prone to apoplexy, even later in life.'

'Perhaps not,' he agreed. 'But when he died, the last Danforth was three years older than I am now. I have held his title for half my life. It is time that I see to securing the succession.'

'True. But I cannot imagine you making a match with any of the girls here,' she said, glancing around the room with a critical frown. 'They are all far too...' She gave a dismissive wave of her hand. 'The incessant giggling sets my teeth on edge.'

'When I first met you, you had a giggle that was perfectly charming,' he said.

'I was twelve at the time,' she reminded him. 'And you were ten and too easily impressed.' She made another sweeping gesture with her fan. 'By the time I made my come out, I had cured myself of such annoying habits.'

'You were truly terrifying,' he agreed. 'And not the least bit impressed by me or my new title.'

'You wanted seasoning,' she said with an affectionate smile.

A decade and a half had given it to him, if one counted the first grey hairs appearing at his temples. He glanced around the room at the current crop of debutantes and tried to work up some enthusiasm for them. Lenore was right. They were all unbelievably young.

But unlike Lenore in her prime, these were easily impressed. Too much so, in his opinion. When he spoke to them, he saw avarice rather than desire. They wanted the Danforth jewel case and the lines of credit on Bond Street where the shopkeepers would bow and scrape to 'Her Grace'. They wanted to sit at the foot of the finest table in England. He was little more than a means to an end.

The knowledge was infinitely depressing.

'Have you at least made an effort to mingle with them?' Lenore pressured, assessing the crowd with a critical eye. 'You cannot be your usual taciturn self. Even if acceptance of your offer is assured, you must make an effort to speak with them.'

He sighed. 'If gentlemen had dance cards, mine would already be full. I have secured a different partner for each one, with not a single break until dawn.'

'Dancing is not as good as conversation,' she allowed. 'But it is the best that can be hoped for in this crush.'

From across the room, they heard a commotion at the door. A dark-haired man was arguing with the footman that they were still two minutes shy of the strict eleven o'clock deadline for admittance. Beside him, a fussy woman in a gown that was ornate almost to the point of being gaudy was searching pockets and reticules for the precious vouchers that would permit them entry. After much hubbub, they located the cards with seconds to spare and handed them over, stepping inside the doorway and allowing the girl behind them to enter as well.

At the sight of her, Benedict's breath stopped in his throat. Surely this was the answer to his prayers, for the young lady they chaperoned was a goddess. At two and thirty, he should know better than to choose a wife for looks alone. But was it such a sin to wish for a tall wife with a trim figure, huge dark eyes, alabaster skin and hair as black and glossy as a raven's wing?

But physical perfection was nothing without proper temperament. The other girls in the room were in awe of their surroundings and excited almost beyond sense. They could not seem to cease giggling and fidgeting, simpering at their parents, their dance partners and each other. They fanned and fluttered about the room like so many brightly coloured birds.

The girl in the doorway was different. The faint smile she wore seemed neither jaded nor frenetic. It was inquisitive without expectation. As her eyes took in the room and the crowd around her, there was the slightest raise of one eyebrow, as if she asked herself, 'Is this really all there is to the great Almack's?' With one glance she had seen her surroundings not as she wanted them to be, but as they were: a poorly kept assembly room that stank of desperation.

Then, as quickly as it had come, the ironic expression disappeared and the polite smile returned. She was too well bred to mock the honour of being here or to spoil the pleasure of others. She leaned forward to comfort her mother, who was near to vapours over the temporarily misplaced invitations and allowed her parents to lead her into the room for an introduction to the patronesses.

'You have noticed the newcomers?' Lenore said, nudging his arm.

'One of them, at least,' he admitted.

'Close your mouth, Danforth. You look like a dying trout.'

He obeyed and then asked, 'Who are they?'

'Mr John Prescott, his wife and daughter Abigail. The husband is the grandson of an impoverished baronet. The wife is a daughter of a cit, with money so new you can smell the ink.' She raised her quizzing glass for a better look. 'The bulk of Mrs Prescott's inheritance came to them recently, which explains their daughter's rather late come out.'

Not too late, in his opinion. An additional year or two past twenty had allowed her beauty to mature and given her the poise he sought in a duchess. Or perhaps she had always been perfection. 'Does Miss Prescott have admirers?' he asked, trying to pretend that answer did not matter one way or the other to him.

'Not yet,' Lenore said, lowering her glass. 'The family connections are nothing to speak of and the parents are…difficult.'

He ignored the warning and concentrated on the lack of competition. The fact should not excite him as much as it did. There were likely a million reasons he should take his time, beyond Lenore's warning. He did not really know this girl at all. And he had been informed on many occasions that he was difficult to get along with. They might not suit.

He was staring, as if he had no manners at all. She had felt his interest and suddenly her gaze fixed on him with the same undisguised curiosity he had been showing her. For the first time in ages, he felt his stomach drop inside him, as if he had fallen from a great height and was unsure of his landing. If he did not get control of himself, an ungentlemanly rush of blood would announce his interest to everyone in the room.

He thought himself far too sensible to believe in love at first sight, but those that claimed it must have felt something very like what he was feeling now. There was a sudden mutual interest that had nothing to do with his title or her pedigree. As he looked into her eyes, he felt a bond form between them that, with time, might become unbreakable.

He looked away again, to compose himself. He would get nowhere gawping across the room at her like an idiot. He had but to walk a short distance across the room and request that Lady Jersey make the introductions. But before he could take a step, the band played the opening notes of a Scottish reel and his first partner tugged at his coat sleeve to remind him of his obligation to her.

He smiled in reassurance and silently damned his early arrival and his conscientious plan to interview every girl in the room. Now that someone had arrived who actually interested him, there was no time left to meet her. Much as he wanted to, he could not turn his back on the promises he had made to his other, young partners. A single dance meant nothing to him, but it was another matter entirely to them.

He took the hand of the girl at his side, offered a brief apology for the momentary distraction and led her out on to the floor. But he hoped she did not notice that, as the patterns of the dance allowed, he stole glances at Abigail Prescott.

The Countess of Sefton was parading a stream of men past her that the patronesses had deemed worthy for introduction. It spoke much of Miss Prescott's estimated value on the marriage mart that they were offering nothing higher than a baron. If and when Benedict expressed interest, he could easily outflank her other suitors.

Or perhaps not. When Miss Prescott had looked at him as she entered, there had been none of the usual rapacity he saw in girls who were trained from birth to grab for the highest title they could get. She had given him one brief glance of assessment, then looked away. She had not given him another thought for the rest of the evening.

The other girls in the room were all desperate to capture his attention for longer than the time he'd allotted to them. As each new dance began and another girl was added to their ranks, his previous partners waved handkerchiefs and smiled, trying to catch his eye as he passed them, complete with the subtle signals from their fans to show their high esteem for him.

But Miss Prescott ignored him. Her utter disregard was more intriguing than any flirtation. He was not accustomed to being ignored.

In turn, she was being passed over by the *ton*. She danced twice. Her first partner was Lord Blasenby, who was a notorious boor. As they stood out at the bottom of a neighbouring set, Benedict watched her nodding patiently at the inanities her partner was pouring into her ear, making no show of being as bored as she probably was. But when the dance ended, Benedict was sure he observed a brief sigh of relief.

Almost an hour later, she stood up with Andrew Killian, the worst dancer in London, and the partner of last resort for wallflowers and spinsters everywhere. After that, she sat along the wall, her mother at her side, her father pacing nearby. They were ignored by the crowd, but not by Benedict, who continued to observe.

Miss Prescott took two glasses of lemonade, but did not finish her slice of cake. He sympathised. As usual, it was dry and flavourless. After a time, another man approached, but seemed to think the better of it, turning away before he reached her side. Benedict expected it was because of the actions of her father. Mr Prescott's bellicose behaviour towards his family would frighten all but the most ardent suitor. As the evening passed and it was clear that his daughter was not a success, he made matters even worse by glowering at all and sundry as if their lack of attention was a personal affront.

Her mother had begun to tremble like a mouse before a cat, but Miss Prescott weathered the storm with ladylike stoicism. Her smile was unchanging, her fan moved in time with the music.

Benedict forced himself to continue smiling at his partner, as his jaw tightened in annoyance. If this was how her father behaved in public, he was likely even worse at home. The girl's admirable control must come from regular practice. It was a skill he wished she'd never had to master. He had always hated bullies. But he truly loathed the sort who would terrorise their own families.

The current set brought him close enough to the velvet ropes separating the dance floor from the seating that he could hear scraps of the family's conversation, though it did Prescott too much credit to call it that. Diatribe would have been a more accurate description of what was being inflicted on the two ladies.

'If you had not taken so long in dressing, we could have arrived on time. And then...'

His voice faded as Benedict moved forward, met his partner, circled and returned to his place.

'Lose the vouchers and leave me stammering at the door...'

He advanced again in an allemande and returned.

'Those gowns cost a pretty penny.'

He moved forward again to touch palms with his lady, then they executed a promenade down the row and up the outside while he seethed beneath his calm. It was beyond vulgar to complain about the price of a lady's dress, especially when the money had come from one's wife. Everyone knew that a lady's Season was expensive, but a good match made up for the cost.

'What are the results so far?'

This was outside of enough. His daughter had shown remarkable grace in what must be her first visit to the premiere assembly room in London. But apparently her father expected instantaneous success, though it was clear to a casual observer that Prescott's bad manners were driving away potential suitors. As Benedict swung past in another turn, he could see Mrs Prescott's lip trembling in what was probably a prelude to tears.

If she broke down in public, the Prescotts would be the gossip of tomorrow. Today, no one would do a thing to stop it, declaring that it was none of their concern. It made his blood boil, for he hated to see any innocent suffer at the moods of an arrogant man. But how best to intervene without causing more talk?

He smiled. In a minute or two, this dance would end. He would be left in a perfect position to help without having to charge across the room like an idiot. Since he would be standing right in front of her, it would look quite natural to request that a patroness introduce him to a newcomer. He knew from experience that even the most stubborn tyrant would be silent in the presence of a peer. An acquaintance with a duke, even though the meeting was a brief one, would increase Miss Prescott's worth in the eyes of the *ton* and assure that she never need be a wallflower again.

Most importantly, she would remember him fondly when he called upon her later in the week.

Another travelling step around the ladies brought him back into position to continue his eavesdropping. And for the first time, he heard her voice, a resonant alto that cut through the tirade like a honey-dipped knife. 'Father?'

The older man emitted a low growl of warning at the interruption.

'Mother is about to cry. If you do not stop hectoring her immediately, I shall make a scene that all of London shall remember.'

His partner nudged him until he remembered that one did not stop dead in the middle of a dance floor to listen in on strangers. He rushed the next steps to return for more.

'A fit, perhaps. Or demonic possession. We shall be banned from more than Almack's when I am finished. No man in England will want me.'

'You wouldn't dare.'

'Would you care to try me?'

Benedict grinned as the pattern of the dance moved him away from the group again. She did not need his help after all. Abigail Prescott was better equipped than he had ever imagined to rescue the night and protect herself and her mother.

Across the set, his partner smiled brilliantly back at him, convinced that he was smitten.

Indeed, he was. The Duke of Danforth had found his Duchess.

Chapter One

Three months later...

Abigail Prescott stood in the entry hall of Comstock Manor, staring down at the puddle of muddy water that had dripped from her skirts onto the immaculate marble floor. It was an excellent metaphor for her interactions with the peerage thus far. She could not seem to stop making a mess of them.

And her mother could not seem to stop apologising on her behalf. 'We cannot tell you how grateful we are for your assistance.' Mrs Prescott's hands fluttered nervously as she spoke and drops of rain water splashed from lace cuffs to baptise the little dog that sat at the Countess of Comstock's feet. 'If there had been any other choice...'

'One cannot predict the weather,' the Countess said with a shrug. She was a plain woman with a matter-of-fact manner. Though she was even younger than Abby, she had the serene composure of a woman twice her age and did not seem the least bit bothered to have a carriage full of wet strangers imposing on her hospitality.

'But to arrive in your home with no introduction...' her mother added, still pretending to be horrified that they had wandered into an earldom without an invitation.

'Do not discompose yourself. Even if your carriage was undamaged, I would not have expected you to return to the village in this storm when my home was in sight.'

The exaggeration was another example of the Countess's generosity. The Manor was almost a mile from the spot on the main road where they had abandoned the brougham, leaning drunkenly on its broken springs. Since she and her mother had got thoroughly soaked during the trudge up the muddy drive to the house, it could have been no worse to walk back down the road to the nearest farm. But her mother had turned towards the luxury of the Manor like a needle to a lodestone and here they were.

'We have interrupted your house party,' her mama said, throwing a wistful glance towards the back of the house and the sound of laughter and conversation.

'You cannot possibly continue your journey until your carriage has been repaired and the road cleared of fallen branches. That will not be possible until the storm has ended,' the Countess replied. 'In the meantime, there is ample space here for a few more guests.'

It was probably true. Abby had got little more than a glimpse of the Manor as they had run towards it, bonnets dipped to the ground to protect against the driving rain. But it had seemed almost ridiculously large, with more wings and ells than could be filled by even the largest party.

'If it is truly no bother...' her mother said, all too eager to be persuaded.

'I will send a servant to retrieve your luggage and a maid will show you to your rooms. However...' The Countess paused. There was a faint smile playing about her lips as though what she was about to say would pay them back for any inconvenience they might have caused. 'I feel it necessary to warn you that the Duke of Danforth is currently among my guests.'

At this announcement, her mother's composure failed and her lip trembled, signalling the beginning of a response that might be far too sincere and more embarrassing than her dripping apologies.

Abby grabbed her hand and tugged sharply, pulling her away from the Countess before she could speak. She felt worse than her mother did about seeing the Duke again, but she was not about to break down in the entrance hall and display her emotions to the whole house. 'Thank you for informing us. I will do my best to prevent any awkwardness.'

'As will I.' The Countess smiled. 'As I said before, it is a very large house.'

Not large enough.

Abby had known that she would have to face the consequences of her actions eventually. But when the moment came, she'd assumed she would have had time to prepare for it. She had not expected that she would come upon him without warning and be unable to get away.

'I will arrange the seating at the table accordingly. You need not speak, if you do not wish to. Or participate in any activities that might force proximity.' The Countess gave an airy wave off her hand to indicate the insignificance of the problems. Then she grew serious. 'But the other guests are likely to gossip.'

Behind her, Mama gave a small yip of distress and the Countess's lapdog whined in response.

'There cannot possibly be more talk than there has already been,' Abby said, reaching into her sleeve for the spare handkerchief she kept for her mother. She turned and offered it, and accompanied it with a warning look to remind the older woman that fussing over the situation only made it worse. Then she turned back to the Countess with a smile. 'We will be fine. And again, we thank you for your help.'

Lady Comstock nodded in return and reached for a nearby bell pull. 'You will feel even better after a hot drink and some dry clothes. Dinner is at eight and I do not want you to miss it.'

When the maid arrived to take them to their rooms, they were led up the main stairs, past the main wing of guest rooms and down a dimly lit centre hallway with threadbare carpet and faded wallpaper. Her mother cast a longing glance over her shoulder at the newer, nicer rooms in the front of the house.

'I am sure these are lovely, as well,' Abby whispered, not wanting to appear ungrateful in front of the servant.

'It does not matter,' her mother replied with a watery sigh. 'We will not have the opportunity to compare accommodations with the other guests. Despite what the Countess said, we shall have to take all our meals in our room.' The maid had opened the door of the first room and Mrs Prescott hovered in the doorway, fluttering in and out like a moth trapped in a chandelier.

Abby walked in without hesitation and smiled at the maid. 'The room is lovely. Please thank the Countess again for her generosity.' The statement was true enough. Though it was clear that it was not in the first tier of accommodation, the linens had been recently aired and the blue silk on the walls and heavy damask curtains on the bed were free of stains or dust. She gave her mother what she hoped was a significant look. 'And I assume you are right next door.'

The older woman disappeared after the maid only to reappear a few moments later through an adjoining door. Before she could embarrass them again with her complaints, Abby glanced into the hall to make sure the maid had gone, then shut the door.

Judging by the look her mother was giving her, she had decided against tears in favour of recrimination. 'Have I not told you often enough that your past misbehaviour would come back to haunt us? Now, when a perfect opportunity to re-enter society has appeared, we have been relegated to the back of the house and kept far away from the rest of the guests like lepers.'

Abby sighed and closed her eyes, trying not to imagine what might be in store for them when they went downstairs again. Just the thought of seeing the Duke again made her head ache. But that was the future and could not be predicted. Here and now, she must calm her mother or she would have two scenes to deal with instead of one.

She opened her eyes again, then put on her most patient smile. 'We have been given these rooms because the best ones have been given to people that Lady Comstock invited to her home. We would not be here at all if you had not ignored my request to return home when the weather worsened. You insisted that we must go on towards London. Now we are trapped and must make the best of it.'

'And if you had not jilted the Duke of Danforth, we might have been invited here in the first place.'

There was some truth to that. But if she had married the Duke like everyone had wanted her to, she'd have made everyone happy but herself. After years of keeping the peace by putting her own needs behind those of the family, Abby had not been able to manage it. 'The Countess of Comstock seems prepared to forgive me on that account. Perhaps, some day, you will as well.' She sat down at the dressing table, removed her soggy bonnet and began pulling out pins so she might properly dry her hair. 'For now, I mean to do as she suggested and prepare for dinner. I have no intention of hiding in my room to avoid one man.' Even if she wanted to, now that they were in the same house, she doubted she could prolong the inevitable meeting for more than a day or two. It would be easier to get it over with quickly.

'Have you no shame at all?'

'I have nothing to be ashamed of. I am not the one travelling about England with a mistress always in tow.'

'Do not be ridiculous.' Her mother tutted. 'You could not possibly do so because you are a young lady.'

Abby sighed again. 'As usual, you are missing the point.'

'I am ignoring it,' her mother replied. 'That is what a decent young girl would do, when given the opportunity to marry a man of such stature.'

'Then I am sorry to be such a disappointment,' Abby countered. 'Despite all your efforts to the contrary, you have raised an abomination.'

It was fortunate that she had not expected a denial after that proclamation, for none came. 'I knew there were too many books in the house. But your father insisted you be educated. And now look at you.'

Abigail smiled into the mirror. 'Despite the rain, I do look quite well today, thank you.'

'You know that is not what I meant.' Now Mama was positively huffing with indignation.

'I am what I am,' Abby announced. Though, in her heart of hearts the fact frustrated her even more than it did her parents. Life would be so much easier if she were anyone else. 'If I could not manage to ignore Danforth's mistress before we were to be married, it would have been just as hard, after. I saved us all from future unhappiness.' In truth, it had been nothing more than a brief reprieve. Despite her mother's belief she was without shame, she had been far too embarrassed

to question the Countess as to whether the Duke had
come alone or brought Lady Beverly with him. Tonight, she might have to face her worst nightmare at
dinner. She would have to share a table with the two
people in England she had never wanted to see again.
At the thought, her stomach clenched. Perhaps she
could excuse herself early, for she doubted that she
could eat a bite, feeling as she did.

'I am more concerned with the past than the future.
The least you could do is apologise to him for the trouble you have caused,' her mother said with a note of
pleading in her voice.

'Since a lady has a right to change her mind, I have
nothing to apologise for,' she replied, ignoring the niggling fact that there had been many less embarrassing
ways to call an end to the engagement. Instead, she
had chosen to make a spectacle of him. She felt even
worse knowing that she had earned any punishment
society decided to inflict.

Her mother deserved some small share as well for
putting her in this situation, so she added, 'I will en-
deavour to avoid him so as not to make things worse.
And, since you were no doubt hoping when we barged
in here that we might find me a husband, I will set my
cap for the first fellow I see on the ground floor. Then
Danforth can keep his mistress and I can keep house
somewhere else. The whole matter will be settled by
morning.'

At this, her mother's lip began to tremble, a signal that her brief show of courage was over. 'Abigail
Prescott, you will not flirt with a stranger under the

nose of the man you spurned. If you humiliate me again, I do not know what I shall do.'

She would probably cry, in public or private. If Abby was the cause of those tears, she would be no better than Father was. She rose and went to her mother, taking her hands and giving them a comforting squeeze. 'I was jesting, Mama. It was cruel and I am sorry. While we are here, I shall be on my best behaviour. Since I refused to marry one total stranger, I promise you I will not be flirting with another.'

'He was not a stranger. He was a duke. Everyone in England knows him,' her mother said with a wail, still mourning the loss of Danforth. 'What more did you need to know?'

'What else could I possibly need to know but his title?' she said with an ironic smile that was lost on her mother.

There were myriad answers to that question. His favourite colour. Whether he preferred coffee or tea with breakfast. If he had a dog. There were a hundred things she wished to know about him that she had not learned. The most important of them was what had motivated him to offer for her in the first place.

She pushed them all to the back of her mind and tried to give her mother a sincere smile of encouragement. 'Since he was not particularly interested in me during our engagement and has made no effort to speak with me after, I doubt he will want to acknowledge my existence, much less trail me around the house interfering in my doings. I am sure we will both feel better if I ring for a maid to get us out of our wet clothes and changed for dinner. Then we will go downstairs and meet the other guests, and I will prove to you that things will not be as terrible as you fear.'

Chapter Two

Benedict stood patiently in the finest guestroom of Comstock Manor as his valet dressed him for dinner. When he'd arrived, the Earl had told him that it was a former repose for King Henry VIII.

He had seen better.

Until recently, Comstock had been an American. It was quite possible that he knew little to nothing about the house or its previous guests and had made the story up out of whole cloth. Still, it was comfortable enough. The mattress was not a Tudor antique and he slept well on it.

'Chin up, Your Grace.'

He obliged as Gibbs flipped the linen cravat about his neck and began the knot.

There was a single knock on the door and, as usual, it opened and closed before he could even give his permission for entrance. He watched in the mirror before him as Lenore crossed the room to sprawl among the pillows on his bed.

'You should not be here,' he reminded her with a sigh. 'Especially not during the day when anyone might notice.'

In response, she laughed in the deep, throaty way that made heads turn and breeches tighten. After twenty-two years of exposure, he had developed some immunity to it. 'Might notice? Darling, I made sure that they did. I would much rather that people think I am with you than that they realise what I really get up to on these trips. I doubt some of them could stand the shock.'

Despite himself, he laughed. The movement of his head earned an annoyed grunt from Gibbs, who tossed away the spoiled neckcloth and went to the wardrobe for a replacement.

He took advantage of the respite to turn from the mirror and address her directly. 'You know that I would never deny sanctuary to a lady in distress, especially when she is my best and oldest friend. But some day, it might be interesting to go on a trip where I do not have to be the last bulwark between you and disgrace.'

She answered with a shrug and a smile, and, as usual, no promise to change in the slightest.

'Do I want to know who you have been visiting when you are pretending to be with me?'

She shook her head. 'It is better that you do not. But my liaison will pale in comparison with the scandal about to break at supper tonight.'

'Do tell,' he said, taking care not to move as Gibbs began the new knot.

'The weather today is as bad as it was yesterday, which is to say, only a bit better than last night,' she said. 'We shall all be trapped inside until the storm breaks and that could take days.'

'I am aware of the fact. The room has windows.' He flicked a glance to the panes which were currently rattling in their frames under pea-sized hail.

'But today, there have been some surprise additions to the party. A fallen tree in the road caused a carriage accident. The travellers are sheltering here until the weather turns and the vehicle can be repaired.'

He turned to glance over his shoulder, receiving a sigh of frustration from the valet, who tossed the second spoiled cloth aside and picked up another.

'Since this is not my house, I have no say in the matter. I am told there are forty rooms. It should not matter at all if a few more people come here.'

'The stranded guests are Mrs Prescott and her daughter.'

Now, it felt like the valet was knotting the cloth tight enough to strangle him and Benedict tugged it away, tossing it down to lie with its fellow before turning to face Lenore. 'Which Prescott?'

'The only one that matters,' she replied, eyes flashing with amusement as she waited for his response.

He had no right to be annoyed. If she had not come to give him a warning, he might have ended up facing a dinner table full of people eager to dissect his reaction at the first sight of his former fiancée. And a fine show he would have given them had he come upon her unawares. Even with advance notice, his initial desire was to curse aloud, his second to run screaming into the rain and try to avoid the meeting that awaited him in the dining room.

Instead, he took a deep breath and apologised to Gibbs. Then, he held a finger in the air to warn Lenore of the need for silence. He ignored her expectant expression and stood stock-still until the valet had completed his work.

He was being foolish. He was used to scrutiny. His title was so old that he tended to be the ranking peer at most any gathering and he had come into it when he was still a boy. It was not unusual to feel all eyes in the room upon him, especially when he was travelling with Lenore.

But his friendship with her was old news. Though people tended to suspect the worst about them, they did not dare to voice their theories aloud. A meeting with Abigail Prescott was another matter entirely.

'It has been long enough since the incident that I doubt anyone will even remember,' he lied, as Gibbs gave his coat a final brushing.

'Do not be naive,' she said with a soft laugh. 'It has been barely three months since she left you standing alone at the altar in St George's. I was in the parlour when the other guests learned of her arrival and the room fairly hummed with the desire to gossip.' She gave a modest bow of her head. 'I came here so as not to inhibit them.'

He gave her a sour smile. 'You might have remained and prevented it.'

'Only delayed it, I am sure.' She shrugged. 'If I do

not allow them some liberties, they will take to avoiding me so they might talk about you in peace.'

'You are willing to sacrifice my reputation for the sake of your own popularity.'

'As I have always done. You have been telling me since we first began going about together that you did not care what people thought of you.' She touched a hand to her ample bosom and gave a dramatic sigh. '*My* reputation was your main concern. What would the world think of me, that I was so much in your company?' Her hand dropped to her side and she looked at him, eyebrow raised. 'It is a surprise to find your chivalry failing just when things are becoming interesting.'

'I was young and foolish back then,' he replied. 'Not that I regret it, of course,' he added, for in truth he did not.

'But you did not think through the repercussions,' she added. 'Nor did you imagine that you would be trapped at a house party with me and your betrothed.'

'My former betrothed,' he said firmly. Then he attempted a joke to change the subject. 'And I chose to keep company with you because I assumed that, eventually, you would see the error of your ways and accept my proposal.'

'Silly boy.' She smiled fondly. 'My opinion has not changed in all the years we have been together. We did not suit then. We do not suit now.'

'Not as you did with your first husband,' he agreed.

'I did not suit him, either.' She laughed.

'But I could not imagine a better union than one between two friends,' Benedict insisted.

'You could not?' She arched her eyebrow again. 'Having tried it, I can assure you, there is more to marriage than that. You need a woman who will give you a son.'

He frowned. 'I thought I had found one.' He could still remember his first glimpse of Abigail Prescott's flashing dark eyes and serene smile. One meeting was all that had been necessary to decide him. In less than a week, they had been engaged. 'It was all arranged.'

'And then she jilted you.' Lenore did not exactly chortle, but there was a distinct lack of sympathy in her tone.

'I gave her no reason.' He was still not sure what had changed her mind.

'Now that she is here, you must ask her.'

He frowned, wishing she would drop a subject that was embarrassing enough without additional commentary.

'You have made no effort to speak to her, thus far,' she reminded him. 'It is time you did.'

'Since we are not married, you have no power to nag me into doing things I do not wish to.' Not even when she was right. His childish infatuation for Abigail Prescott had been accompanied by equally childish anger at her rejection. Perhaps she was in love with another. Perhaps the responsibilities involved in elevation to Duchess were too daunting.

Or perhaps she simply did not like him.

But she could have been polite enough to inform

him of the fact in person or in writing before the actual ceremony. He had thought it wonderfully brazen when she'd threated her own father with a public scene. But it had been another thing entirely when she had pulled the same trick on him without the courtesy of a warning. If she did not want to marry him, then he had no intention of chasing after her to beg for a reason. If the girl was a harpy in the making, then their failed wedding had been not so much an embarrassment as a reprieve. If she could treat him thus before the wedding, then their marriage would not have been the peaceful union he sought. It would be misery from start to finish.

As the days turned into months, he had decided the less he thought about her, the happier he was likely to be. Now she had appeared out of nowhere to destroy what small amount of peace he had managed to regain. But that did not mean he would give her the satisfaction of seeing him hurt. Having witnessed the results of unfettered emotion in his family, he would not give her the satisfaction of seeing him lose control.

He stared into the mirror, pretending to admire the beautifully tied cravat to show how little this supposed crisis mattered to him. Then he turned to Lenore. 'If she wished to ruin her reputation by crying off, it was not my business to ask why. Nor do I mean to offer her any more than I already have. If a dukedom is not enough to get her to the altar, I cannot imagine what she expects.'

'It could have been nothing more than fear on her

part,' Lenore said in a gentle voice. 'You can be quite intimidating when you set your mind to it.'

He laughed. 'Do you think I bullied her into marrying me? She is lucky that I took her on at all. With a philandering drunk for a father and a social-climbing cit for a mother, her family pedigree was not likely to gain her an offer as good as mine.'

'It did not seem to bother you at the time,' Lenore replied. After a lifetime's acquaintance, she could look through him like an empty glass.

'And it does not bother me now,' he insisted. His last comment had sounded like the petulant outburst of a man who cared far too much. 'If you wish to know the truth of her motives, you will have to ask her yourself. When I see the girl, I mean to treat her in a civil manner to prove there are no hard feelings on my part. But I am not going to beg for an answer, nor will I be goaded into a public confrontation for the amusement of the crowd.'

Her lips formed an 'O' of astonishment and she looked ready to question him further. He had few secrets from Lenore, but friendship did not entitle her to pick through the remnants of his heart like a rag bin. 'Gibbs, please see Lady Beverly out. If she spends another minute meddling in affairs which do not concern her, she will not have time to dress for dinner.'

His valet went to the door, opened and stood respectfully to the side and gave Lenore the patient look that servants used when forced to obey commands that were not likely to go well.

Lenore looked between master and servant, then

laughed. 'Putting me out?' She rose from the bed as gracefully as she had taken to it. 'You have never done that before.' Then she swept past him and through the door, turning to leave a parting shot. 'This will be an interesting—'

At Benedict's signal, the door closed before she could complete the sentence.

Chapter Three

It did not take long for the Comstock servants to prove that there had been no insult intended in the rooms they had been allotted. Before Abby and her mother had finished speaking, a string of footman appeared, carrying their luggage from the carriage, and Lady Comstock's own maid was hurrying between their two rooms, drawing baths and pulling dinner gowns from their trunks.

An hour later, with her hair dried, curled and decorated with emerald pins to match her green silk gown, Abby felt more than a match for anything or anyone that might await her on the ground floor. But upon arriving there, it took only a moment to realise that things were not as bad as Mother had expected—they were far worse.

Their appearance in the door of the sitting room brought the action within to a sudden halt. It was as if she was staring at an oil painting of the *ton* at leisure and not an actual party. All chatter stopped. Glasses paused halfway to lips and, though play had stopped, hands around the card table rose slightly to disguise the curious expressions of the players that held them.

Beside her, she could feel her mother begin to falter. She sympathised, for she could feel her own heart racing wildly and her blood pumping ice through her veins. Before either of them could make things worse by showing their fear, Abby pushed from behind, forcing her mother forward. Once they'd passed the threshold, the Countess bore down on them with the singlemindedness of a dreadnought. 'Mrs Prescott, Miss Prescott, please, come join us.' She kissed their cheeks as if they were old friends and not complete strangers, then forced her way between them, linking arms and towing them into the midst of the gathering. 'Even if it comes from misfortune, I welcome your company. You are not yet acquainted with my husband. We must remedy that immediately. And if there are people in our little group you do not know, point them out and I will be happy to make introductions. I am sure all are as happy to see you as we are.' Then she swept the room with a steely glare that was in opposition to her honeyed tone, as if daring anyone to go counter to the wishes of the hostess.

With a rustle of satin and a few nervously cleared throats, the other guests offered forced smiles of welcome, turning away as soon as they could find an excuse to return to what they had been doing before the Prescotts arrived.

Before they had a chance to be bothered by it, the Countess had them across the room and standing in

front of the Earl of Comstock, who complained about
the miserable English weather and assured them that
everything would be done to make up for the discom-
fort it had caused. Though he'd held his title for over
a year, his temperament and accent were still somewhat colonial. But at least there was no trace of the
reserve Abby sometimes felt when people were confronted with her mother's unguarded emotions and
unpolished manners. It did not seem to bother him in
the least that she had not been born to associate with
someone of his rank.

Unfortunately, the latitude of their host encouraged
her mother to speak her mind in the worst way possible. 'You are too kind, my lord,' she said with a giggle.
'But if you are sincere in saying you will do anything
to make us comfortable, there is one small thing…'

'Anything within reason, Mrs Prescott,' the Earl
said, with a playful glint in his eye.

'Might you arrange to introduce my daughter to any
single gentlemen who are here? She is still husband-
hunting, you know, and I shall not truly be at ease until
I see her well married.'

Would that the rain had drowned them before they'd
made it up the drive. This was a level of embarrassment
that Abigail had never imagined as they had forced
their way into this house. Only an hour or two ago,
her mother had been threatening to hide in her room
and insisting that Abby not shame herself by flirting.
But now she was all but auctioning her off to the first
man who would take her and expecting a peer to be
a panderer.

'She is already acquainted with one of your friends, Comstock. But I doubt I will be of any help.'

On second thought, she did not wish for a watery death outside. She wanted the floor to open beneath her right now and swallow her without a trace. She did not even have to turn around to know that the Duke of Danforth had heard what her mother had said and inserted himself into the conversation.

This was not what she'd expected at all. As she'd dressed for dinner, she had been steeling herself for a cut, direct or indirect. When they finally met, she was sure he would ignore her for as long as he could. If forced to face her, he would look through her, then turn away.

It would be embarrassing, but survivable. She would pretend that she had not noticed. She would speak to everyone else in the room, laugh and talk, and act just as she would if he had not been present. After a few hours of misery, she would be able to go back to her room and gather the strength to do the same thing to-morrow.

Instead, the Duke was standing right behind her and making a direct reference to the embarrassment she had caused him. Though every nerve in her body demanded that she run, she turned slowly to face him.

He was wearing the same distant expression he had worn on the first night she'd seen him. It was not quite a smile, but neither had it been a frown. Though he ate and danced and chatted with the other people in the room, he had seemed to exist apart from them, as if listening to a voice that no one else could hear. In Almack's she had thought it sad and felt a sudden, deep sympathy with him, wondering what might he required to ease his burden.

It was only later, as the wedding had approached, that she had suspected the truth. Ordinary people bored him. He wore an entirely different expression for those closest to him and she was not included in that number.

Now he seemed to be mocking her. Let him do it. If she was to be extricated from the mess her mother had just made, she could see no other way forward than to throw herself on the Duke's mercy and hope for the best. So, after giving a nervous smile of recognition, she eased herself free of the Countess's grasp and dropped in a respectful curtsy. 'Your Grace.' As she dipped, she kept her eyes trained on the floor, staring at the toes of his well-polished boots and praying that he would give her some hint as to what she should do when she rose again.

He must have been wondering the same thing, for she could swear she felt the weight of his gaze, like the brush of cat's tail against her bare skin.

Or perhaps that feeling of heaviness was the attention of the other guests. The silence in the room had returned, as even the Countess waited with bated breath to see how he would respond to her greeting.

And then, the mood was broken by the deep, feminine laugh of someone who was unaware of the excitement occurring on the other side of the room. Abby raised her eyes and watched all heads swivel to find the source.

She did not have to follow them for she was sure

who she would see. As she'd feared, if Danforth was here then Lady Beverly would not be far away. And as she had from the first moment she had learned of the woman, she wondered why the Duke had even bothered to propose to her when he already had such a woman at his beck and call.

Lenore, or Lady Beverly, was several years older than the Duke, though her looks gave no indication of the fact. Her hair was gold to complement the copper of his, her eyes a clear ice blue. But there was nothing cool about the smile on her full, pink lips, nor the womanly curves of her body. Though Abby had been more than a little pleased with her own appearance when gazing into the bedroom mirror, the feeling was forgotten when she looked at Lady Beverly. She was nothing compared to such a woman.

Even worse, the relationship between this goddess and Danforth was the worst-kept secret in England. All of London declared the two perfectly suited and wondered why they hadn't married years ago. The most popular theory held that the Marchioness was barren. Lady Beverly had been married for almost a decade and was now a childless widow. No matter how charming and attractive, a woman who could not conceive would be completely unsuitable for a peer in need of an heir.

But the absence of children made her even more qualified for other, less proper activities. Several of the men in the room were looking at her with more than cursory interest, as if hoping that it might be possible to sway her affections, should the Duke displease her.

But a change of loyalty did not seem imminent. As she turned to Danforth, she sparkled like a diamond, overjoyed that he was in the same room.

Then she was moving towards them, still smiling as if equally pleased to see the Prescotts. Abby barely had time to rise from the curtsy before she was enveloped in a cloud of scent and an almost tangible aura of bonhomie.

'Danforth.' The name reached them in a husky whisper as she grew close. 'Is this she?' Her expression was somewhere between curiosity and avarice, making Abby feel more like an object than a person. 'She is as lovely as you said.'

It would not have been possible for Lady Beverly to remain ignorant of the engagement, which had been announced in *The Times*. But the thought that she had been a topic of conversation between the lovers made Abby's stomach knot in horror. If they had expected her to ignore their extremely public relationship, the least she had been owed from Lady Beverly was a similar feigned ignorance should they ever meet.

Then, insult was added to injury as the woman said, 'Benedict, you must introduce us.' She expected the look on Lady Beverly's face to betray the irony of her request. But there was no trace of mockery in her smile. Its delight seemed genuine, as if she truly had been waiting an age for this meeting.

Even worse, Danforth did not seem the least bit surprised by it. Only a few moments ago, he had been ready to protect her from embarrassment. Now he did not hesitate to say, 'Lady Beverly, may I present Mrs John Prescott and Miss Abigail Prescott.'

Her traitorous mother, who had never been able to resist a title, abandoned the last of her pride and curtsied to the Duke's woman as if there was nothing the least bit wrong about it. Then she gave Abbey a pointed look, as if she expected her to do the same.

It proved just how little she knew about her own daughter. She had walked away from the most successful match of the Season, to avoid this exact moment. She could feel the entire room watching her, analysing her every move, searching for any clue to her thoughts. As she did when dealing with her father, she forced her face to remain impassive and unreadable.

But her body's response was much harder to control. She could feel her palms grow clammy and fought the urge to wipe them on her skirt, since the act would only embarrass her more. Though the room was lit by candles, it suddenly seemed impossibly bright. The glare burned into her brain making her head feel both unbearably heavy and dangerously light. If she did not do something, and quickly, she was destined for complete humiliation. She would be sick, right in the middle of Lady Comstock's ornate Aubusson rug.

So, she did as she had planned to do, months ago, in London when she had spent weeks in dread of the meeting that had now finally occurred. Without another blink of acknowledgement to either Lady Beverly or the Duke, she looked through them as if they did not exist, turned and walked away.

* * *

She had done it again.

Had it been insufficient to making him a laughing stock in London? She had tracked him to the country so he might watch her hunt for a husband before their uneaten wedding cake had had a chance to stale. He had been ready and willing to make peace with her. He had even made a joke out of the comments of her ill-bred mother. But instead of accepting the olive branch he offered, she had cut him dead.

Of course, Lenore was partly responsible for how badly this first meeting had gone. If she had allowed him a few moments to speak with the girl before sailing into the midst of their conversation, things might have gone better. But once she took a mind to meddle in his affairs, Lady Beverly was a force of nature. Avoiding her help would be almost as challenging as forging a truce with Abigail Prescott.

Right now, Miss Prescott was sitting down the table from him, making polite conversation with the lady next to her. The only indication that she remembered the scene she had made in the sitting room was the way she refused to acknowledge Lenore, who was sitting directly across the table from her. All around them, people were trying to pretend that nothing of interest had happened while eavesdropping to see if it might happen again.

It was a pity that Lenore had not decided the same. While she did not speak directly to Abigail, she had no such qualms about talking to Mrs Prescott. She complimented the woman on her lovely daughter and listened with fascination to the dramatic story of their arrival at Comstock Manor. It did not seem to bother her one whit that Miss Prescott had walked away from her offer of friendship. In fact, it seemed to intrigue her. She had turned to Benedict after Abigail had left them and whispered that the girl was indeed perfect for him, insisting that she would fix everything.

Benedict did not want things *fixed*. If he did not want to make things even worse, the best course of action was to do what he did best and maintain an unruffled demeanour, showing no signs of the anger seething inside.

It did not help that Abigail Prescott was even more beautiful than she had been three months ago. Then, his fleeting feelings of desire at the sight of her had made him feel slightly guilty. To want a woman because of her appearance was not unusual. In some ways, men were still little better than animals. But to be thinking of one's future wife in such a way seemed somewhat immoral.

So, he had tricked himself into believing that he was attracted to her spirit. The audacity of her response to her father had not been admirable, as he'd first thought. It was probably a symptom of misandry. Pity the man who finally succeeded in marrying her. He would be treated as she had treated Benedict: as the butt of a joke.

But now, even after he had learned the truth, he could not stop thinking about her. When he had seen her in the sitting room before dinner, polite conversation had been the last thing on his mind. Just as it had been in London, he had wanted to see her dark eyes hooded in pleasure, her white throat stretched in yearning and her red lips parted in a gasp as he thrust…

Such thoughts were unseemly. To prevent them, he had seen to it that their contact before the aborted wedding had been minimal. The few meetings they'd had had been well chaperoned to avoid any hint of impropriety. His manners had been impeccable. He'd given her no cause to treat him as she did.

But now, like it or not, here she was. And although the other guests were too polite to speak within earshot, he could feel the gossip in the air like eddies in the water of a pond. Everyone was waiting to see what would happen next.

He felt a certain curiosity about the matter himself. He knew what he wanted to do…had wanted to do since the fateful day at St George's Church when he had stood, shifting from foot to foot beside the bishop as he had waited in vain. Then he had imagined going to her town house, kicking in the door, throwing her body over his shoulder and hauling her back to the church.

Tonight, a similar fantasy gripped him. It began with spilled wine glasses and shocked guests and ended with her sprawled naked on the wide mattress of the Tudor bedroom, begging him for marriage or anything else he suggested.

But that was not the end. Only the beginning.

Instead, he sipped his wine in silence, staring down the table to where the ladies were seated.

'Comstock Manor is a very large house.'

Benedict started at the comment, which appeared to be directed at him, then focused his gaze on his host, the Earl of Comstock, and did his best to appear attentive. 'Indeed.' He paused for a moment to select the correct compliment for the situation. 'It is most attractively arranged.'

'It is a damned nuisance under most circumstances,' the Earl replied. 'We spend all our time patching the leaks in the roof. But it is fortunate to have the extra rooms when one has a sudden influx of guests. There is a whole wing beyond the central one that is totally empty, save for the Prescotts.'

Benedict gave the Earl a much sharper glance this time for it sounded almost as if he was giving directions to Miss Prescott's bedchamber. 'I am sure they are glad of the privacy,' he said in a warning tone.

It had no effect on the Earl, who was gazing blandly into the baked apple that had been set before him. 'Should they wish for even more solitude, they have only to proceed further down the wing. It turns, you see. If one does not get lost, one ends up far out of sight and hearing of even the most inquisitive servants.'

'How interesting.'

'Beyond that, there are stairs to the main floor and a plethora of rooms we have not bothered to open for this party.'

When Benedict did not respond, he added, 'If I wanted to speak to my Countess—or engage in any

other activity I did not want the house to know of—
I would consider exploring the back of the house.'

'I assume you are suggesting that I speak with Miss
Prescott,' he said, frowning at the Earl to show him
how little his advice was wanted.

'Speak with her,' Comstock repeated, with a sigh.
'If talking is all you wish to do, then I encourage you
to do so. But first, I suggest you listen to her.' He
stared down the table at Abigail. 'She looks like a lady
with much to say.'

Chapter Four

'That went well,' Abigail said, as she held the taper aloft to light their way down the long corridor to their rooms.

'Sarcasm is not a virtue in young ladies,' her mother said, peering into the gloom. 'I have had far too much of it from you already.'

'I was not being sarcastic,' Abby replied. It was more an outright lie, as was the smile she'd pasted on her face so she might look sincere. 'I was quite satisfied with the outcome.'

'You alienated yourself from a lady who is esteemed by the Countess and her guests. You will find Lady Beverly to be quite charming, should you decide to speak to her.'

When put that way, it sounded almost reasonable to accept Lady Beverly's friendship. Since things between herself and the Duke had come to a permanent end, the presence of his mistress should not really matter at all.

And yet it did. It still hurt to think of the two of

them together, smiling and laughing, and even worse, doing the private, secret things that men and women did together. The rest of society might be able to forgive the charming Lady Beverly for her disgraceful behaviour. But they had not spent weeks wondering if the man they were to marry would stay with them long enough for the bed to grow cold.

But there was no point in living in the past or the future. To maintain her fragile peace of mind, she must concentrate on the present. She forced herself to smile at her mother, opening the older woman's door and lighting a candle at her bedside. 'You must console yourself on one point, at least. I will not be able to do anything else disgraceful until morning. Now, ring for your maid and get a good night's rest, Mama. You will need all of your wits about you to mollify whomever I manage to offend at breakfast.'

Her mother's mouth opened, ready with a scold. But before she could manage it, Abby had exited her room and shut the door after her. She leaned her back against the panel for a moment, listening to the sounds beyond until she was sure that her mother was settled. Then turned to go to her own room.

Suddenly, there was a scrabbling and clicking of nails on the oak floor of the hallway and the little black and white dog she had seen earlier came trotting out of the darkness towards her.

'Hello, little fellow,' she said, stooping down to pat him. 'Have you been sent to guard our rooms? I do not think you are big enough to prevent a liaison, should I choose to have one.'

The idea was both bold and optimistic, since her public fall from grace had gone past the point where a man might consider her seducible. Even a rake would think she was more trouble than she was worth. But the little dog seemed to like her well enough and wagged his tail as he worried the toe of her slipper.

'Be careful,' she whispered. 'They are silk and cost me all of five pounds.'

The dog was clearly unimpressed by the warning. When he looked up at her, he had a ribbon rosette clenched tightly in his teeth.

'You little beast. Give me that before you ruin it.' Then, as she usually did, she opted for rash action instead of discretion and lunged to grab him.

The dog proved too quick for her, darting between her outstretched hands and running further down the hall, pausing at the edge of the candlelight. There, he dropped the ribbon on the floor and offered a lopsided doggy grin of challenge.

'I am not playing,' she said, walking towards him more slowly this time so as not to startle him. 'Give me that flower.'

His tail wagged slowly from side to side like a Maelzel metronome, timing her approach.

She slowed and the tail stopped, the little legs of the terrier tightening for a sprint.

'Good doggy.' It was a lie. Judging by the narrowing of his little black eyes, even the dog knew that. If she could not manage to make nice with the Countess's guests, the least Abby could do was try to befriend her horrible little dog.

But not to the point of sacrificing a shoe. She ran the last few steps towards him and made a grab for the rosette. Her fingers touched the drool-damped silk for only a moment, then the dog grabbed it and tore down the hallway deeper into the house.

She ran after him, her candle waving wildly in her hand to light the way. In a house of such enormity, she would never see the thing again should she let the dog out of her sight. There were too many beds and sofas to hide it under and acres of lawn to bury it in.

Ahead of her, the dog reached the end of the corridor and went skidding around a corner. She hurried to catch up, turning to the right, then pulled up short. Halfway down the hall, the glow from a single candle revealed a man blocking the way. The dog was sitting in front of him, wagging his tail as if seeking a reward for the decoration that had been dropped at his feet.

Even before she could see him clearly, she had no doubt as to who it was. When lit by candles, the Duke of Danforth's skin had a golden glow about it, as if he had been cast in bronze. The faint glints of copper in his hair that matched the flecks in his verdigris-green eyes only added to the illusion.

That first time she had seen him across the crowded room at Almack's, he'd been so still and quiet that she'd imagined that someone had draped a burgundy wool coat over a metal statue. He had been a little too large and a little too perfect to be a living, breathing man.

Then, an equally inappropriate thought had struck her. Would the comparison to well-cast bronze hold, should he remove his garments? Without shirt and breeches, would she be able to find some flaw in him? Would he seem small and ordinary? Or would he have the deeply ridged muscles of a Poseidon, the commanding presence of a naked god?

Then she'd realised that he was looking at her.

Perhaps her speculation upon his person had been obvious on her face. For just a moment, his composure had slipped. Though he'd made no effort to cross the room, he had stared back at her, the rest of the room forgotten. Their gaze had locked for what seemed like hours. And then he had turned back to the woman next to him, offering a quiet aside and a last glance in her direction.

Lady Beverly had looked at her as well. Then, immediately back to him, offering information.

He had asked about her.

She had looked away, momentarily shaken by the attention, and enquired of the patronesses who he was. After learning that he was the ranking peer in the room, she began to hope that the night might not be the disaster she'd been fearing.

But nothing had come of it. As the hours ticked by, he had not come to speak to her. He'd not enquired as to the huge gaps in her dance card or the fact that her hands were empty of refreshment. He had not made even the most banal comment about the closeness of the crush, the quality of the music, or the beneficence of the hostesses. So, she had forgotten him.

At least, she had tried. Since he was a duke, he was not the sort of man it was possible to forget.

A week later, he had come to the Prescott town house to speak to her father. And before she had understood what was happening, she was engaged to him.

Now, he was staring at her out of the darkness with the same impenetrable expression he had worn that night, watching her approach without a word of greeting.

'What are you doing here?' she whispered, glancing around her to be sure that they were not observed.

'Waiting for you,' he said in a normal volume. The statement was accompanied by a bland look that implied the answer was obvious. 'The Countess assured me a meeting would be arranged.'

If her idea of an invitation was to send that annoying little dog, then perhaps it had been. It had been surprisingly effective. Had the Countess of Comstock suggested that she come to an isolated part of the house to speak to him, she'd likely have refused. 'What did you wish from me?' she said at last, then waited for him to explain himself.

His answer came without polite preamble. 'I suspect you are eager to get away from here. In the morning, my carriage will be at your disposal. You may be on your way before breakfast has ended.'

It had been too much to hope that he'd wanted to apologise for his part in the embarrassment before dinner, but she had not thought that he would be so eager to be rid of her. There was some consolation in his bluntness. She was far too annoyed by it to feel nervous. 'Why wait for morning? I will wake my mother and we can be gone immediately.'

There followed a moment of silence that seemed to last an eternity. 'You are mocking me,' he said, at last. 'It is pitch-black and pelting rain.'

'How perceptive of you to notice,' she said.

'The weather, or the mockery?'

His riposte threw her off balance, for it had almost sounded like a joke. But it could not have been, for she had yet to see evidence that Danforth had a sense of humour. She blinked, marshalling her thoughts. 'The weather is fearsome. I know, because I came in from it just a few hours ago. Do you have some prescience about tomorrow that you can assure me that the roads will be any more passable or the journey less of a threat to my safety?'

When he did not immediately reply she added, 'Or do you simply want me to go away?' The worry she felt in the ensuing silence was strange, for there was no reason to fear his answer. If she had cared what he thought of her, she should have found a less public way to cry off.

'I thought I made it clear enough, when I offered for you, that I desired your company.' Though she heard no trace of sarcasm in his voice, she was sure it was there. 'You were the one to leave me. I am merely giving you the opportunity to do so again.'

Though it should not have, his frank assessment hurt. Some part of her had hoped he was angered by her departure. She had wanted him to feel something, anything at all, over the loss of her. But there was no indication that it mattered to him at all. 'I will leave when it is sensible to do so, with or without your help,' she replied. 'At the moment, the roads are inches deep in mud and were near to impassable even before our accident. Once the rain has stopped it will be several days before they are dry enough to be driven on.'

He considered the fact for a moment, then nodded his acceptance. 'Very well. If departure is impossible, we must learn to make the best of our time together and avoid any more unfortunate incidents like the one before dinner.'

'When you attempted to introduce me to your mistress?' she said, not bothering with subtleties.

'When you snubbed a marchioness, who has been welcomed and befriended by your hostess,' Danforth corrected, in the patient tone one might use on a child. 'Lady Beverly has no problem with you and is eager to be your friend. If you expect the other guests to take your side in a feud of your own creation, you will be sorely disappointed.'

'I expect nothing of the kind,' she insisted.

He raised an eyebrow, then shrugged. 'Then I shall put it down to a flair for the dramatic and a youthful tendency to act without thinking of the consequences.'

'And now you are referencing the end of our sham engagement,' she said, feeling a tiny spark of the anger she had felt in the weeks before the wedding.

'A sham?' Now, he seemed more puzzled than angry. 'I offered in all sincerity.'

'Not to me, you didn't,' she replied.

'I distinctly remember speaking to you on the matter,' he said, his brow furrowing. 'We met in the salon of your family's town house. I offered and you accepted.'

'What else could I do? The whole matter was settled before anyone thought to involve me.' Now, the single flicker of irritation was growing to something much more like rage. 'You spent more time talking to my father than you ever did to me. The day of the wedding arrived, and I realised that I had not seen you since the day you made the offer. But my father had spoken to you at least a dozen times.'

'We share a club,' he said absently.

'And we were to share a bed,' she snapped.

For the first time since she'd met him, the façade of perpetual ennui disappeared and she saw real emotion on his face. His eyes darkened to the deep green of the sea in a storm and his lips parted in a smile that had nothing to do with mirth. Then, he moved closer until she could feel the heat of his body through the air between them. 'Yes, Miss Prescott, after our wedding, I would have taken you to my bed. But a meeting of bodies is one thing and a meeting of minds is quite another. I had hoped that, after some time together, the latter would develop from the former.'

'And I hoped quite the opposite,' she said, surprised. 'It cannot be possible to enjoy the marital act with a complete stranger.'

In response, he laughed. And something deep inside her trembled in answer to the sound. 'Would you care to wager on the fact?'

'It is likely different for men,' she added, taking a steadying breath to counter the odd sensations that the question evoked.

'In a way, perhaps.' He placed a hand on the wall beside her head and leaned even closer, until she felt his breath at each word. 'In my experience, it matters little whether the woman is a friend or a stranger. But for a woman?'

His voice grew soft until it was barely more than a whisper. And against all modesty, she leaned closer to him, so she would not miss a word.

'The pleasure of the act has much to do with the skill of the partner. I can assure you, Miss Prescott, you would have had nothing to worry about.'

Then he reached for her. And without another thought she closed her eyes and waited for his kiss.

When it did not come, she opened them again, feeling like the foolish young girl he seemed to think she was. He had not been about to touch her. Instead, his fingers rested lightly on the holder of her candle, steadying it to keep her trembling hand from dropping it.

He nodded, confident that he had proven his point. 'I believe we have reached an understanding on one thing, at least. When we see each other tomorrow at breakfast, I trust that there will be no more embarrassing scenes. If we can bump along together for a few days in peace, this whole unfortunate incident will be over and we need never see each other again.

Goodnight, Miss Prescott.' Without another word, he stepped away from her and proceeded back down the hall towards the occupied portion of the house.

At her feet, the black-and-white terrier sneezed as if to remind her of his presence. Then, after one final snuffle at the silk rosette, he trotted after the Duke, leaving her alone.

Chapter Five

The next morning, Abby rang for a maid to bring chocolate and toast to her room. It was the same meal she would have taken at home, therefore it was almost honest to claim that the choice had nothing to do with a fear of whom she might see in the breakfast room of Comstock Manor.

Since he'd shown scant desire to talk to her thus far, she doubted that the Duke of Danforth meant to comment directly on her behaviour in the hall the previous evening. But if he wished to speak to others of the complete and utter looby she had been, she hoped he would use the time she had allotted him and be done by the time she came down stairs.

Of course, he might have informed Lady Beverly of it immediately after he'd left her. Abby could imagine the pair of them, sharing a pillow and laughing at how lucky it was that he had not been trapped into a permanent union with such an idiot. Though she had hardly managed a bite of last night's dinner, she pushed her plate away and set down her cup, unable to eat. She was unsure what part of that picture bothered her most, but she was sure that Lady Beverly never had to beg for kisses. If she had wanted one, it would have been given immediately.

There was a sort of dismal satisfaction in the realisation. Abby's presence here would have little to no influence on whatever was happening between the Duke and his lady. Though her embarrassment was acute, they were so far in each other's pockets that they had probably forgotten all about her by now.

If anyone else cared about her, they were likely to gossip more if she kept to her room than if she went downstairs to face them. If she sulked upstairs all day, she would worry herself into a state over nothing at all. The wisest course of action was to do what she'd told her mother she would do. She must get dressed, go down and join in whatever activities were planned for the day.

It appeared that the morning's entertainment was nothing to be frightened of. Judging by the sounds of laugher ringing down the halls, the gentlemen were enjoying their game in the billiard room. The ladies were gathered in the morning room, listlessly picking at needlework or writing letters that could not be posted until the weather cleared.

As Abby entered, heads rose, eyes blinked and minds seemed to consider whether whispering about her was even worth the effort if the Duke was in another room. She tensed for a moment, then heard a collective sigh of boredom as almost everyone returned to what they had been doing.

Then she noticed Lady Beverly sat at a table across the room, shuffling cards in preparation for a game of patience. The riffling stopped and she set the deck on the table with a final snap. Then she rose, directed her brilliant smile at Abby and started towards her.

That single smile was all it took to destroy her calm. Abby glanced around the room in desperation, searching for her mother or anyone else who might provide a rescue. She could feel the beginnings of a megrim starting at the prospect of another meeting with the Marchioness. There had to be someone else she could talk to, instead.

'The Countess has taken Mrs Prescott to the library to find a book,' Lady Beverly said before she could even enquire. 'I will escort you to her.'

Abby considered responding with another snub, then decided to accept the information as the perfect reason to escape. 'The library,' she repeated with a stiff smile. 'Thank you for the information. An escort will not be necessary. I will find her myself.'

'Nonsense,' the other woman replied, her smile widening. 'The house is large and difficult to navigate. Let me help you.' There was a strange urgency to the last words, as if she thought she was the one who could provide the rescue that Abby wanted and not the thing she had needed saving from.

Before she could refuse again, Lady Beverly's arm was linked with hers. 'Come. Walk with me. We have so much to talk about.' The grip might have looked sisterly to the other ladies watching, but it felt like an iron manacle as it pulled her out of the room and down the hall.

Abby had a brief and misguided urge to struggle free and run. But if the Marchioness did not intend to leave her alone until she had been acknowledged, it would be easier if their meeting took place away from the prying eyes of a dozen gossipy women. Talking with the Duke alone in the hallway had raised any number of strange desires in her. But even so, it had been easier than making polite conversation in the sitting room. Perhaps solitude would make the current interview less awkward.

Once they were clear of the room, Lady Beverly loosened her grip and gave Abby an affectionate pat on the arm. 'Alone at last, Miss Prescott. You have no idea how eagerly I have been waiting to talk with you.'

'I thought I had made it clear to you when we first met that I had nothing to say to you,' she said through clenched teeth, resisting the urge to strain back towards the morning room like a dog on a leash.

'Nonsense,' Lady Beverly replied, still smiling. 'We have Danforth in common. And that is all the world.'

'Not to me,' she insisted, wishing her voice sounded as convincing as Lady Beverly's. 'If you recall, I ended our engagement months ago.'

The other woman smiled and arched an eyebrow. 'If you are really done with him, then you have no reason to dislike me.'

The Duke had said as much, last night. There was a certain logic to the argument, but it overlooked one important point. 'I do not wish to associate with you, because I was raised to believe that ladies did not so-cialise with…' She left the sentence unfinished, hop-ing that it would not be necessary to explain.

'With girls so far beneath their station?' Lady Bev-erly said with a laugh. 'Do not worry, my dear. If you are good enough for Danforth, you are good enough for me.'

'*Was* good enough,' she snapped, forgetting the problem at hand. 'The engagement is over.'

Lady Beverly's smile turned sympathetic. 'Of course it is, Miss Prescott. And just now, I was only teasing you. I know exactly what you were hinting at and what you must think of me. You are young yet, my dear, and still have the shine of idealism. The rules you describe are commonly ignored when there is suf-ficient money or status involved.'

'Not by me,' she said, slipping her arm free. But now that she could leave, she did not want to go until she had made herself understood.

'Of course, your convictions have nothing to do with your feelings for the Duke.' The woman nodded, with a sceptical quirk to her smile.

'I feel nothing for him,' she said firmly. 'I barely know him.'

'If that is true, then there is no reason we can't be friends,' Lady Beverly said, nodding again as if the matter was settled. 'You must call me Lenore.'

There was a conversational gap where Abby was expected to offer a similar latitude. When she did not, Lenore continued. 'I would not blame you if you did harbour a lingering penchant for Danforth. He is magnificent, is he not?'

It was impossible to argue with this, so again, she said nothing.

'You are a lucky woman to catch the eye of such a man.' Abby could find no trace of irony in the woman's tone, but neither did she hear envy. The words almost sounded like approval and that made no sense at all.

She shook her head, rejecting them. 'There was little more to his side of our engagement than expediency and likely a hundred other girls in London who might have suited as well.'

'And yet he chose you. He feels more deeply than you know,' Lady Beverly said in a low voice.

'How can you tell?' Abby blurted, before she was able to stop herself.

'Because I am his oldest friend,' the other woman replied. 'He spoke frequently of you during the brief period between the offer and the ceremony and expressed his hopes for the success of your marriage.'

'I do not like being the topic of other people's conversation.' Though it was some small comfort that it had not been the mockery she had assumed, the idea brought forth small stirrings of the anxiety she'd felt in the weeks leading up to the wedding.

'Then I can see why you might have hesitated to marry a duke,' Lenore said and this time her nod was approving. 'You must realise that, no matter what your union is like, people cannot seem to help gossiping about the titled men who run our country and the women they marry.'

'I do not care what most people think of me.' Perhaps if she said the words often enough, she would come to believe they were true. But even now, she could not help wondering what the ladies in the morning room were saying about them in their absence. 'And I expect any man who, as you put it, cares deeply, would bring his thoughts and concerns to me, rather than sharing them with another woman.'

If possible, Lenore's smile grew even more brilliant. 'You are jealous.'

'Of you?' She had hoped that the words would sound scornful and put the Marchioness in her place. But they came out weak, revealing that she was all too aware that if this was a competition between them, she had lost it in the very first move.

'I knew that was the problem. Danforth refused to acknowledge that our friendship would be a difficulty. Men, even when they are great and powerful, can be terribly naive when it comes to the hearts of the women around them.'

Abby smiled in amazement at the woman's audacity. 'Your friendship?'

'You think it is a polite euphemism,' the woman said, with another smile. 'But it is not. We are friends. Nothing more.'

'It does not concern me, one way or the other.' She stopped just short of disproving the statement by telling Lady Beverly that it was far too late to waste the energy to lie about such a thing.

'I am glad to hear it,' Lenore replied. 'And do not trouble yourself that Danforth has not declared himself.

I know him better than he does himself and can assure you that he is a surprisingly sensitive soul.'

'Really,' Abby said, unable to let such a monumental falsehood pass. 'I have met stable doors with more tender feelings than he has shown me.'

'You could blame his father for that,' Lenore replied. 'The elder Danforth was prone to rages that reduced his family and servants to tears. He saw emotion in others as a weakness and proof of his own strength. The impassivity that his son cultivated must have been maddening.'

'How unfortunate for him,' she replied, not wanting to feel the rush of kinship as she thought of her own father's rants.

'It was indeed. That is why I am so happy he has found someone who will understand him,' Lenore said, opening the door in front of them. 'And here is the library. Is it not every bit as awful as I said? Let us collect your mother and go back to the others.'

When Benedict returned to his room after breakfast, it was to find Lenore ensconced in the pile of pillows on the bed and reading a book. She set it aside and looked up expectantly.

'Don't you have somewhere else you wish to be?' he said, glancing into the hall before closing the door and wondering how many people had seen her arrive.

'Nowhere nearly as interesting as this,' she said, smiling. 'I have spoken to Miss Prescott.'

He passed an exasperated hand over his face. 'Did she speak to you in return?'

'A little,' Lenore said, obviously quite pleased with

herself. 'She is consumed with jealousy over our relationship.'

'We do not have a relationship,' he reminded her.

'That is what I told her. When you offered for her, you should have told her the same,' Lenore said, shaking her head.

'Polite young ladies should not be listening to gossip, much less believing it.' It sounded like the sort of judgmental nonsense her parents would have told her, had she objected to the match. 'I meant to explain,' he said. 'But I thought there would be more time.' Instead, he had lied to himself and said nothing at all to her.

'After her reaction to me last night, it should have been clear to you that some action was necessary,' she said, obviously exasperated.

'I spoke to her about it,' he admitted, wishing that the conversation could end there so that he did not have to admit what a fool he had been.

But now Lenore was staring at him as if she was surprised that he had not told her every last detail of the exchange immediately after it had happened. 'I offered her the use of my carriage to depart and she declined. I reminded her that you are an honoured guest here and cautioned her to refrain from further ill-mannered behaviour towards you, then we parted company.'

'After three months of silence, that was all you could manage?' Lenore's mouth gaped with an incredulous smile. 'To tell her she was rude and that you wished her to go away?'

'I was angry.' He had told himself that, because he was not shouting, he was in complete control of his temper. But a half day later, his suggestion that she go sounded both cruel and petulant.

'That would be a surprise to her. She still thinks you care nothing at all about her,' Lenore said, rolling her eyes.

'I am not very good at being angry,' he admitted. It made him feel even more foolish than the attempt had been.

'Considering the lessons you had from your father, you should be a master of invective,' she replied. 'Did you at least learn why she broke from you?'

'It was clear from our conversation that she had expected a level of intimacy in our early associations that I would not have been comfortable with.'

Lenore laughed. 'Even if you have become a monk without telling me, I doubt you have forgotten your previous sins. What could a young lady of good character possibly desire that you have not already experienced and enjoyed?'

'And you are clearly no nun, that your mind immediately turns towards such ideas,' he replied. 'She complained that I did not talk to her. She feared that the lack of communication between us during our betrothal was proof that the impending union would fail.'

'She noticed that it would be easier to pull your teeth than to get conversation out of you?' Lenore replied.

'That is an exaggeration,' he replied. But the silence that fell between them proved it was the truth.

After what seemed like an eternity, she replied, 'We converse easily because we have been doing it for years.'

'I suspect, after some time in her company, I should have grown accustomed to speaking with her, as well.'

His friend sighed in response. 'And until that time, you expected her to live in silence, with not a hint as to the workings of your mind.'

'That is the way most wives live,' he replied. 'You would not have needed my friendship had you spent your evenings conversing with your husband.'

'Perfectly true,' she conceded. 'You might also remember that many of our early conversations focused on how unhappy I was and how little time I spent in mourning him when he passed.'

'You were not happy,' he agreed. 'But I suspect that your husband was quite content with you. Had he not been, he would have told you so.'

'So, you have been assuming all this time that I was the problem?'

'Not a problem,' he said with a smile. 'You merely sought something in your marriage that was out of line with the norm. For example, I do not see Comstock sharing every intimate thought with his wife.'

'Because the pair of them are simpatico. They hardly need to speak at all.'

'And my own parents…'

'Are hardly an exemplar. Your father was a bully who made both you and your mother miserable.'

'I am sorry I told you of it,' he said, for this made his point perfectly. 'Now that you have the information, you are using it against me to win an argument.' That was the risk of sharing too freely. It gave the other person an advantage.

She was staring at him again, probably waiting for him to admit that he had missed the entire point of courtship. He had been seeking a helpmeet. But instead, he had treated Abigail Prescott like an adversary.

'She said I spent more time talking to her father than I did to her,' he said, remembering one of her other complaints.

'And what did you think of that man, when you met him?'

'I wanted to save her from him.' He smiled in satisfaction, remembering how quickly John Prescott's bluster had faded when he had realised the purpose of Benedict's visit. 'It was amusing to see how easily cowed he was when speaking to his betters instead of his family.'

'I am sure he took any perceived slights out on them when he returned home,' she replied.

'I asked for her hand and he ordered her to marry me.' Now that he had discovered it, the truth was so glaringly obvious as to blind him to everything else.

'And you assumed she would be overjoyed that the man she hated most in the world had found her a husband,' she concluded, with a huff of disgust.

Since no one would dare refuse a duke, she'd had no choice but to accept him. Once she had, he had thought the matter was settled. He'd given her no chance to discuss their future together, or to withdraw from the engagement. It had forced her to refuse in a way that did not need words. She had made a public spectacle of their wedding, just as she had threatened to do at Almack's.

'I handled the offer badly and the engagement even worse,' he admitted at last.

'And what do you mean to do about it now?' Lenore said with another pointed look.

He had no answer. Her rejection of him had been justified. But it was also the sort of scandal that might permanently ruin her chances to make a decent match and earn her a lifetime of recrimination from her parents. An apology on his part was hardly sufficient.

Then he remembered her on the previous evening, so close he could almost taste her. She had been every bit as lovely as she had been in London and even more spirited. He had not been able to resist provoking her, tempting her until she had closed her eyes and swayed towards him, ready to accept his kiss.

Then, like a fool, he had walked away from her. At the time, he'd congratulated himself on resisting her charms. Now, it seemed more like a wasted opportunity. But until the rain stopped, they would be trapped here together. And, as Comstock had pointed out to him at dinner, the house was very large and rife with possibility for clandestine meetings.

'What am I going to do?' he said, feeling his face relax into a genuine smile for the first time in ages. 'I am going to do what I should have done in the first place and pay proper court to Miss Abigail Prescott.'

Chapter Six

That night, as they prepared him for dinner, Benedict instructed Gibbs to take unusual care with his appearance. The comment seemed to surprise the valet, either because his work was never less than his best or because his master rarely expressed his opinion on it.

When they were completed, Benedict offered his thanks and Gibbs responded with a dazed, 'You are most welcome, Your Grace.' If his manservant felt undervalued, it was yet another reminder of the need to speak aloud his opinions, to avoid misleading others.

Either way, the result was the same. When he entered the main salon where the guests had gathered before dinner, female heads turned and he heard more than one sigh of admiration. But there was no reaction at all from the corner where Abigail Prescott stood, speaking to her mother. Her back remained turned to him, though she must have known he had entered the room from the expressions of those around her. It annoyed him to note that she was as lovely from the behind as she was from the front. Though her mother's gown was overloaded with lace and ruffles, Abigail had chosen a simply cut gown of scarlet silk, without so much as a gold chain to spoil the elegant sweep of pale skin from the neckline to the black curls piled on her head. Though some might have thought the gown's colour too bold for a young lady, the contrast changed her skin from flawless white to luminous opal.

She looked well and, by the faint half smile on her face as she turned to look past him, she knew it. The other men in the room noticed as well. He could see the interest in their eyes and the quick sidelong glances in his direction as they tried to decide if he was still interested in her.

If they continued watching, they would have their answer tonight. The real question was whether her interest in him was stronger than the spark of physical attraction he had seen last night in a darkened hallway. For now, he watched her from across the room, not wanting to give her a reason to retire early and avoid him. When the time came to process to the dining room, he took his place of honour near the head of the line, while she and her mother stayed near the end.

As it had been last night, the table was organised in the rather old-fashioned seating that kept the men and women separated at opposite ends of the table. From his place near the head, he had ample opportunity to watch her try to evade Lenore's attempts at conversation. She needn't have bothered. It was nearly impossible to resist the force of Lady Beverly's personality when she decided to inflict it on one. It would have been an exaggeration to say they talked with the ease of old friends, but by the end of dinner Abigail had answered several of the lady's questions and smiled at least once.

And rather than pushing her food around the plate as she had at last night's dinner, he saw her finish both her soup and her fish, and at least half of the sorbet brought for the dessert.

After dinner, he sat as patiently as possible through the fine port and deadly conversation of the other gentlemen, until Comstock deemed it time to join the ladies in the card room. The ladies had already arranged themselves at various tables and he spotted Mrs Prescott and Abigail seated together near the fire. Then he took advantage of his rank and outstripped the other men in the group to take the chair he desired. A single raise of his eyebrows was all it took to warn off a competitor for the spot opposite his former fiancée. When the fellow adjusted to take the chair opposite Mrs Prescott, Lenore slipped in ahead of him, favouring him with a smile that would melt glass. 'I hope you do not mind, sir. But you have interrupted the most interesting conversation with Mrs Prescott, just now.'

'About the weather,' Abigail supplied with a deadpan expression. 'Apparently, it is raining.'

Benedict offered her a sympathetic smile. 'Indeed.' He looked to Lenore, offering a silent signal that her help was not needed. But she was suddenly absorbed in shuffling the cards and dealing out a round of casino.

'A penny a point?' Mrs Prescott asked. Then, her eyes grew bright and she fumbled in the pocket of her gown and removed a thick fold of banknotes. 'Or shall we make the game more interesting than that?'

For a moment, Miss Prescott's expression was one of undisguised embarrassment that her mother felt the need to carry money around with her when visiting a private home. Worse yet, she was looking around her in horror, aware that the other tables were betting with buttons from their sewing baskets or keeping score with pencil and paper. No one was using money at all, much less making sizeable bets. She shot her mother a warning look, badly disguised by a pained smile. 'I am afraid I have left my reticule in my room, Mama. I have not so much as a penny on me.'

'That is all right, dear.' Her mother split the pile of bills in half and offered some to her. 'I have enough for both of us.'

'Playing for money. This shall be interesting,' Lenore agreed, beaming at the three of them as if she had never gambled before. Then her face fell and looked to him with an expression that would move a heart of stone. 'But I never carry money while in the country.'

He was about to suggest that she find a different table, for, with or without money, she was a terrible card player. But before he could speak, Miss Prescott threw herself on the statement as if it was a life raft after a shipwreck. 'What a shame,' she said in a tone far too cheerful to match her words. 'If one of us has no stake, we cannot possibly play.' She was halfway out of her chair and reaching for her mother's hand, ready to drag her away, before she had even finished the sentence.

Benedict reached for her other hand to stop her from going. 'Do not fear, Miss Prescott. I am sure I can find a few pounds to lend my friend.' He knew instantly, that the gesture had been a mistake. Other than a brief caress months ago, when he had slipped the betrothal ring on to her finger, he had never held her hand before. Now that he had started, he did not want to stop. It was a lovely hand, not precisely delicate, but just the right size to fit easily, should she choose to turn it over and clasp his.

But she did not choose. The look she was giving him was not quite panicked, but it was clear that his touch had embarrassed her. She sank back into her chair, weak with shame and he felt her hand slide away from him and disappear into her lap.

'Thank you, Danforth, darling. I can always count on you.' Lenore was touching his other arm in the casually affectionate way she often did to support their ruse.

But for the first time in ages he was tired of pretending. He shrugged away from her touch and searched his coat pockets and found a handful of crumpled pound notes tucked into the tail. He flattened them against the edge of the table, then pressed half of them into the hand that had been caressing his sleeve. 'When you lose this, which you most certainly shall, you are done for the evening.'

Lenore accepted the money, kissing it for luck before setting it back on the table, and picked up her cards so that play could begin.

Miss Prescott was a surprisingly astute player. At

first, she seemed to ignore Benedict, just as she had over dinner. She collected spades, built and discarded, and made sure that there was nothing left on the table for her mother. The older woman was consistently left with the lowest number of points in the round and a rapidly vanishing stack of notes.

She did not need to bother treating Lenore in a similar manner, for that lady was quite able to lose on her own without other players having to strategise against her. In only a few hands, the two weakest players at the table had run out of blunt and Mrs Prescott was looking wistfully at the money her daughter was holding. 'I have more in my room, if you would be willing to wait but a moment.'

Before Abigail could censure her, Lenore spoke. 'Must we really play another hand? This game grows quite tiresome after a while. And I do have the latest issue of Ackermann's fine magazine waiting for me in my room.'

'I have not seen that, as yet,' her mother said with a sigh.

'You shall see it now, if you wish. And you must admire the new ballgown I had made from it. The fabric is straight from Paris. And the lace…' Lenore raised her eyes heavenwards.

It took no further temptation to make Mrs Prescott forget her cards and the two ladies left the table and strolled arm in arm out of the room.

Now that they were alone, an awkward silence fell between them. Miss Prescott gathered the cards, shuffled and stared across the table. 'Another hand, Your

Grace?' But her unsmiling face and the impatient snap of the cards as she shuffled announced that she had no desire to play with him.

'Still angry with me?' he said quietly.

Surprised, she lost control of the cards and half the deck scattered on the table between them.

'I do not blame you,' he said, gathering them up and handing them back to her. 'When we spoke last night, I behaved abominably.'

She looked up from the cards, eyes wide with confusion, then glanced around her to be sure no one had heard him speak.

'I was not much of a fiancé, was I?' he said, still smiling.

'You were a duke,' she whispered, so softly that he could barely hear it.

'I still am,' he replied.

She was staring down at the cards instead of looking at him, as if she was using them to see the past instead of the future.

'I know you would prefer it if I simply leave you alone. But if I do, the others will think it a snub. It will create even more talk than continuing to play with you. We have been having such a delightful time together, thus far.'

She raised her eyes from the cards and gave him a look of such scepticism that he had to laugh.

'Come, Miss Prescott, it has not been as bad as all that. You have been winning. Let us see if you can take the last of my money.'

A smile flickered on her lips for a moment, then

she looked down and shuffled the cards again. 'If we are deep in play, it might stop you from making polite conversation with me.'

'It is worth trying,' he said, smiling back at her. 'Your deal, Miss Prescott?'

She passed the deck to him. 'I yield to you, Your Grace.'

Had she chosen those words to distract him? The thought of her, yielding…willing… His mind clouded and he lost the next hand. And the one after that. She had been a smart player before. But now that it was just the two of them, she was merciless. Her face gave nothing away to tell him what she held in her hand. In less than half an hour, the sum total of his pocket money was stacked neatly in front of her.

He tossed his remaining cards on the table, then gathered the rest and reformed the deck. 'You have done well for yourself, Miss Prescott.'

'Perhaps I should make my living as a gambler,' she replied, counting out the bills in front of her without looking at him.

'I doubt your next fiancé will approve,' he said.

She glanced up. 'You speak as if you know his likes and dislikes. Do you know his name, perhaps? Because I am as yet unaware of it.'

Apparently, her mother had been in earnest when mentioning the search for a husband. If she had prospects, she could have mentioned them now, but did not. He shrugged, pretending to be indifferent about her future. 'All men think much alike, Miss Prescott. They do not wish their wives to enjoy cards too much.'

'Even if they win, Your Grace?'

'Even the best gamblers cannot win every game,' he reminded her. 'To assume otherwise suggests the kind of overconfidence that is the reason for prohibition.'

She waved a hand as if to clear away his objections. 'Then it is likely good that we did not marry for I doubt we'd have suited. I do not like to be dictated to.' She shuffled the cards. 'Would you like to play another hand?' Then she gave a moue of sympathy. 'Wait. You cannot, for I have taken all your money.'

He smiled back and patted his pockets. 'So you have. But do not let that stop you. My credit is good, as is my word. Will you accept my marker, Miss Prescott?'

'You do not approve of women who gamble and I do not approve of men who continue to do so when they have no money,' she said, setting the deck aside and preparing to rise from the table.

'Wait.' He had no intention of letting her go, just as things were getting interesting. On a whim, he stripped the ring from his finger and dropped it on the table. 'I suspect this should more than cover the contents of your purse.'

She stared at it for a moment in disbelief, then whispered, 'That is your signet.'

'I am aware of the fact,' he replied.

'That is a symbol of your dukedom. You cannot risk that in a card game with a stranger,' she said, staring down at the ring as if he had dropped a poisonous spider on to the green baize between them.

'I would hardly call us strangers, Miss Prescott.

As you reminded me last night, we very nearly shared a bed.'

She glanced around her to be sure none had heard before speaking softly. 'I would prefer you not speak of such things in a common room.'

'I will not be quiet until you acknowledge that this is a trinket compared to what I have already offered you when I gave you my mother's betrothal ring.' If he didn't want the whole room to hear their conversation, it was good that he could not manage to sound as angry as he felt. The memory of that ring, delivered to his town house in the afternoon post without a single word of explanation, was just as sharp and painful as the day it had happened.

She must have realised his true feelings. By the stricken look on her face, it had never occurred to her that the ring he'd given her as a pledge had held any real meaning to him. 'I am so sorry.' The words were a whisper so faint that it hardly carried across the table to him.

Now that he had his apology, he was not quite sure what to do with it. 'Never mind it,' he said gruffly, reaching for the cards. 'Our engagement is long over. But tonight, I will say when we are through and that time has not yet arrived. I wager my ring against all the money you have before you.'

'But...'

While she tried to think of another objection, he dealt the cards.

It took only one look to remind him what happened when one allowed emotion to gain the upper hand over

rational thought. While making bold statements about
the insignificance of his dukedom when compared to
his heart, he had not accounted for what he might do
with a near-unplayable hand.

*You lost the ducal signet in a card game with a
pretty girl?* He could almost hear his father raging
in his ear.

*No, Father. It was a beautiful girl. And I did not
even bed her.*

He could not help but smile at the thought and saw
the furrow it caused on the face of his opponent. She
thought he was pleased with his cards. How wrong
she was. But there was not much to do but make the
best of them.

And Abigail, God bless her, lacked the ability
to play badly and let the peer win. Even though he
doubted she wished to take this prize, she was not able
to be less than her best.

The warmth that this revelation engendered was
surprising. When had earnestness and sincerity come
to feel like such a novelty? Being abandoned at the
altar had been insulting and embarrassing. But at least
it had been honest. In some small way, it had been as
bracing as a cold bath.

Or a slap in the face. If he had taken to betting the
entail on a whim, he needed a good slap to knock some
of the self-importance out of him.

After a final draw and discard, she laid her cards
in front of her to display the sets. She did not look
particularly happy to be winning, but she had won
all the same.

He laid down his cards as well and pushed the ring across the table to her. 'Congratulations, Miss Prescott.'

'What am I to do with this?' she said, even more dismayed then before and looking around to be sure that the other guests were occupied with their own games.

At a nearby table, Miss Sommersby had noticed the lull in their play and her head was turning in their direction. Before she saw the ring, he seized Abigail's hand, covering it with both of his and closing it in a fist around the signet to hide it. Tomorrow it would be all over the house that he had been holding hands with Miss Prescott. But at least no one would think he had given her another ring. 'Put it in your pocket with the rest of your winnings,' he said, trying not to move his lips. 'It is not large. I expect it will fit.'

'But after that...'

'Take it out on special occasions to show your grandchildren. You can tell the boys of the dangers of gambling and the girls of its advantages.'

'Take it back,' she said, extending her arm to try to push it back across the table.

He released her hand and folded his arms across his chest. 'I knew the risks when I wagered it.'

Then her hand dropped into her lap and out of sight. She tipped her head to the side and stared at him, trying to puzzle out what his actions might mean. 'Then you are a fool,' she said at last. When her hand reappeared, it was empty.

'Perhaps,' he admitted. 'But it is not the first time I have been a fool for you. I doubt it will be the last.'

She stood and he rose as well, bowing to her. 'Thank you for a delightful game, Miss Prescott.'

'Your Grace.' She dipped a convincingly respectful curtsy. But when she raised her face to look at him, though her mouth was smiling, her eyes were wishing him to perdition.

Before she could say another word, he abandoned the card room for billiards.

For something so small, it was very heavy.

Or perhaps it only seemed so because of the burden of guilt. The ducal signet of the Danforth line might as well have been a lead bar. As she moved through the room pretending to observe the other games, she was always conscious of the weight of it in her pocket, bumping against her leg.

He should not have bet it. When he had, she should have refused. She could have at least had the sense to lose on purpose. If not that, she should have walked away and left it on the table, knowing that he would not abandon it to strangers. But he had told her the origin of the betrothal ring he had given her before and she had forgotten everything else.

That tiny piece of gold had been oppressively heavy as well, the weight a constant reminder that she had sold herself to a man who did not care about her. Each day she'd worn it, it had grown heavier. The pain in her head had grown as well. Her stomach had twisted and roiled until she could hardly stand the sight of food. By the day of the wedding, the morning light shining into her bedroom had been agonising, sharp as knives.

But the moment she'd pulled it from her hand, she'd begun to feel better. She'd taken no great care in returning it since she'd assumed it had no real value to him. If it had, he would not have wasted it on a girl he'd barely met.

Had it been a message that she meant more to him than she knew? When he had proposed to her, there had been no indication that he held some secret *tendre*. Her father had introduced them and then left them alone together. Before she'd had a chance to grow accustomed to her first unchaperoned hour with a gentleman, she was engaged. The Duke had not bothered to go down on one knee as she had girlishly imagined a man proposing might do.

The Duke of Danforth did not beg for anything, especially not the love of a woman. The minute they were alone, he had walked to the fireplace and placed his hand on the mantle. It had almost looked as if he'd needed to gather his courage. Then he had turned and explained the situation in a tone that brooked no opposition. He had already requested and received her father's consent. The only thing that remained was for her to answer him.

She had stammered out an acceptance, too shocked to think of anything else to say. And from somewhere close by, she'd heard a door click shut. There had been no sighs or sobs or accompanying huffs of exasperation, so it could not have been her mother. The door had been closed instead of slammed, so it could not have been her father. One of them had sent a maid to spy on the event and make sure that she had done the right thing.

She thought of that door often during the next three weeks as the banns were read. She dreamed of it, closing and locking with her on the inside, trapped. It would not open until the day of her marriage. Then, Danforth would exchange the betrothal ring for the wedding ring and take her to a different house, with more doors and more locks.

She had escaped. But now, months later, he'd tricked her into taking another ring from him. Absently, she tucked her hand in her pocket to make sure it was safe and slipped it on to her finger. It was so large that it slid off again immediately. If she had wanted to wear it, she'd have to close her fist tight, just to keep it from rolling away.

It was a trap of some kind, she was sure. He wanted something from her, but she had no idea what it could be. She could find no explanation for his willingness to risk it, nor could she understand his lack of remorse when he'd lost. For a moment, her mind spun the wild fancy of a cursed ring. But that made no sense at all. The Duke of Danforth, with his wealth, health and stature, was as far from a cursed soul as a man could get.

The way he had spoken after was even more confusing. He had said that she'd made a fool of him. Had he been expecting her to apologise again for jilting him? If so, he'd been none too clear about his wishes. Though she was sure he'd been angry when he mentioned the betrothal ring, he'd shown no rancour when he left her.

As he'd announced that she'd made a fool of him, the calm smile never left his lips. It was as though being made the talk of the Season was little more important than the current weather.

And then, at last, she saw what he had done. It would not be long before someone noticed that he was not wearing his ring. No one would dare ask him what had happened to it. But they would speculate. There would be no stopping the gossip. And it would not be long before someone realised that he'd had it at dinner, but that it had been gone after playing cards with Miss Prescott.

He had tricked her into taking it, knowing that someone, some day, would realise it was in her possession. People would think her a thief or a fortune hunter. He would be seen as the victim and she as some sort of temptress who kept the Duke of Danforth dancing on a string.

She had not thought him a cruel man. In truth, she had not thought he'd cared about her enough to be so. But he could not have devised a more devious punishment than to hand her a ring after she had refused to accept one in church. The first scandal would never die away if he meant to keep bringing it back into the public eye whenever he saw her. Just the thought of it made her ill.

She would not stand for it. She would sneak it back to his room tonight, before anyone noticed it was gone. At the moment, he was still playing billiards with the Earl. If she made a show of exhaustion and announced she was going to bed, she could go to his room and drop the cursed thing on his nightstand. He could not exactly force it on her again, once she had returned it. And she would not be so foolish as to sit down at cards with him again so he might play the same trick.

The idea gave her an immediate rush of relief, which she disguised with an exaggerated yawn and announced that she meant to have an early bedtime, excusing herself from the room. Once on the first floor, she glanced around her to make sure the halls were empty. Then, instead of following the corridor towards the back of the house and her room, she turned to the left and went all the way to the end of the hall where she had been told the best guestroom lay.

It was a relief that he had left the door unlocked, for she'd had no plan if he had secured it. Nor did she know what to do should she see the valet. It was unlikely he would believe her should she claim to be lost. Was he the sort who would keep his master's secrets, or would there be rumours about her in the servants' hall that might spread to the guests?

But no problems materialised. She opened the door to a large room that was well lit and empty. It certainly looked grand enough to house a duke, with crossed swords over the mantel and a heavy oak bedstead carved with Tudor roses. But before she left one of Danforth's most precious possessions here, she must make sure that it was the right room and not simply the room she assumed was right. She needed evidence that it was his.

But the space was so tidy that it was hard to know if it was occupied by anyone, much less the house's ranking guest. There was not so much as a hairbrush sitting out on the dressing table, or a book beside the bed to assure her that she was in the right place.

There was, however, a wardrobe. She had but to open the door and look inside. The coats would be labelled for him by the tailor and his linen was likely embroidered with his crest.

Once she opened the door, she did not even have to look for proof. *She knew.* She was enveloped in a distinctive combination of bay cologne, shaving soap and the delicious underlying scent that was uniquely his. For a moment she swayed on her feet, leaning towards it, just as she had towards him on the previous evening. Then she succumbed and buried her face in the sleeve of the nearest coat.

A man so odious had no right to smell so good. She knew this coat well, for he'd worn it when he had come to make his formal offer to her. On that day, she had been unable to look him in the eye. She had stared at these buttons and memorised each stitch in these lapels.

She released a shaky breath and imagined how it might have been had he loved her. These arms would have held her as she murmured her acceptance, pulling her close to kiss her hair and assure her that he was the happiest man in London. She would have reached around him and hugged him, just like this. She closed her eyes and wrapped her arms around his coat, pulling it from its peg and holding it close.

Behind her, a man cleared his throat.

She dropped the coat and whirled around to see the

Duke standing in the doorway of his room, watching her embarrass herself. The apology stuck in her throat. Once she started it, she doubted it would ever stop, until she had included the acceptance of an engagement that she had not liked or wanted. Their relationship had been a sorry mess from the moment it started and it had been her mistake not to end it before it had begun.

Before she could form the words, he had crossed the room and seized her with such force that she was almost lifted from the floor.

Swept off my feet.

She had heard the phrase but had never given it much thought until it was happening. It was like being caught in a gale and knowing that, since it had been her own foolishness to take herself out in the storm, she could not be overly surprised when it blew her down. He caught her and lifted her as if she weighed no more than his empty coat. Then he was kissing her.

And she was allowing it, just as startled as she was on the day he had proposed. But it was not the gentle kiss she had imagined while hugging his coat. He was kissing her like a man with expectations, opening her mouth and delving into her as if he meant to join them for eternity.

She was supposed to object to this. She should fight, or perhaps she should strike him. But she could not seem to manage the proper reaction. Instead of turning her head, she was answering his kiss with careful thrusts of her tongue, trying to mimic what he was doing to her. She was gripping his arms, not to push them away, but because she wanted to feel the muscles of them, bunching as they held her. As she did so, the ring that she had still been holding slipped from her gasp and thumped to the carpet at her feet.

The sound was not loud, but apparently, it was enough to break the mood. The Duke pulled away and set her gently back on her feet. Then, he stared down at the signet between them and back to her. 'You came to return the ring.'

'I thought you were still in the billiard room,' she whispered.

He ran a harried hand through his blond hair and uttered a curse, then added, 'Of course you did.' He inhaled deeply as if about to say something, then let the breath out slowly before adding, 'I misunderstood.'

Was that what it had been? He had kissed her because he'd assumed she'd come for an assignation? If that was what he had been offering in giving her the ring, perhaps she should be insulted. But she was sure he had not expected her to come into his room and begin riffling through his possessions. There was no way to explain what she had done, since she did not fully understand it herself.

'My fault,' she whispered at last, thinking it all sounded rather like they had bumped into each other in the hall and not been passionately kissing just moments before.

He reached down and picked up the ring, slipping it on his finger with an absent gesture, then walked past her as if she did not exist, going to his bedroom door and opening it to look up the hall. Leaving the door ajar, he walked towards the central hallway, checking in all directions and down the stairs before hurrying back to her. 'There is no one about. No one will see you leave. There will be no awkward questions.'

She had not considered what she'd have done if she had been discovered exiting his room. It was thoughtful of him to do so. It had never occurred to her that there was some sort of etiquette involved with romantic liaisons. But, of course, he would be as well versed in that as he was in all other courtesies. He was a peer, after all. As an inferior, she found his aloof and dismissive nature maddening, but it had never been out of line with good manners.

She had an inappropriate desire to laugh. She would sit down on the end of his bed and ask him if he could see the absurdity of their interactions thus far. Perhaps, if she was honest with him, he would sigh in relief, relax and show his true self to her.

He would think she had gone mad. He was standing in his doorway now, staring at her expectantly, wondering why she hesitated to leave since she had accomplished what she'd come for. Only a wanton would want to remain with him, after he had kissed her without permission. If she stayed, that was what she would be. She gave another quick nod of thanks and hurried from the room.

He looked down the hall after the fleeing girl, waiting to be sure she had rounded the corner by the stairs without incident. He closed the door, taking care to make no noise that might alert someone dozing in a neighbouring room, turned and sagged against it, breathing in, out, in, out, until his heartbeat returned to something closer to normal.

He had behaved just as he'd feared he could on the day he proposed. He had pounced on her like a wolf on a lamb, leaving no time for seduction, or even enquiry as to whether his attentions might be welcomed. It had been wonderful. Even sweeter since he was sure that this had been her first real kiss. Just the thought made his body leap to think of all the other delicious firsts they might have in store.

He took another deep breath. He should have known that there was a logical reason for her to be waiting in his room. Young ladies of good family did not go sneaking from room to room at house parties, bedding and being bedded. Her presence in his had been caused by his provocative actions at the card table.

But that did not explain what she had been doing inside his wardrobe, all but making love to his tailcoat. He had stood in the doorway watching, surprised, amused and perhaps just a bit envious of the wool pressed against her face. He had been wrong to kiss her. But her behaviour had to mean something and he refused to believe that it was some bizarre fascination with bespoke tailoring.

She wanted him. She dreamed of him. She had been willing last night. Tonight, she'd made no effort to resist his kiss. She had responded to it. He sat on the bed. It was not much to go on with. But it was more than he'd had this morning. The seemingly impenetrable defence she'd raised against him was much weaker than it looked.

As he glanced towards the window, a flash of lightning split the sky, making the drops of rain on the window glitter in the darkness. Suddenly, the boredom of a country house in foul weather seemed less like a punishment and more like an opportunity. If the rain held for a just few more days, the future might be much brighter than he'd been expecting.

Chapter Seven

'And then she showed me her jewel case. Her rubies are magnificent! Since I did not bother to bring mine, she thought I might borrow them to wear with my gold gown tonight.'

Abby sighed and closed the book in her lap, unable to concentrate over the torrent of words rushing from her mother. 'I am glad you find Lady Beverly to be such wonderful company. Did she happen to mention if any of her jewels were a gift from Danforth?'

Her mother gave a gasp of disapproval and looked around the morning room to see if anyone had overheard her comment. Fortunately, it was too early for most of the guests to be about and they were able to talk in private. 'We did not discuss anything of the kind.' Her mother was whispering, even though they were alone. 'If you have any feelings for me at all, you will not say such a thing again.'

For a change, her mother was probably right. For as long as Abby could remember, the ladies of the *ton* had mocked her mother for her birth and gauche sense of fashion. But it appeared that the Marchioness was treating her mother warmly, without scorn and with no ulterior motive. They had few enough friends. It was a mistake to refuse a kindness, even when it came from someone she did not wish to like.

'I am sorry,' she admitted. 'It was a petty, horrible thing to say and I will not repeat it.' But she could not seem to stop thinking it.

'Since you are no longer engaged to the Duke, you must learn to make peace with his habits,' her mother reminded her. 'It is no business of yours who he keeps company with.'

That was perfectly true, as well. It should not matter to her who the man bedded. Or kissed, for that matter. Except that he had kissed *her* and she had lain awake half the night thinking of it. What would have happened if he had not noticed the ring? Would he have kept kissing her? How would it have ended? The scenarios she'd imagined had left her whole body tingling and eager to see him again.

And then, when she had left her room to come down for breakfast, she had seen Lady Beverly hurrying down the hall towards the top of the stairs. But she had been wearing the same gown she had worn on the previous evening. The lady had noticed her as well and had the audacity to wink and hold a finger to her lips to indicate silence. Abby turned her head away, not wanting to see where the lady had come from, or where it was she was going to. But it was clear that she had not spent the night in her own bed.

If Lady Beverly had been with Danforth, it was

proof that it had taken him no time at all to forget the kiss he had shared with Abby. She ought to take a page from his book and forget it as well. She simply wished he was not so shamefully obvious about the fact that it had meant nothing to him.

'Abigail!'

She started and looked at her mother, who was staring at her impatiently. 'You are wool-gathering again. I asked you if you have any of the crimson silk in your sewing basket.' She held up the embroidery she had been working on. 'I need a bit of something to finish these flowers.'

'It is in my room, Mama,' she replied, getting up. 'I will bring it.'

As she passed the open door of the breakfast room, she saw Lenore heaping eggs on to her plate and commenting to the Countess, 'I am absolutely ravenous this morning.'

'Due to your rapacious appetite, I am sure,' said Mr Naismith from the other end of the table.

A normal person would have taken offence at such a remark, since the man's tone implied that he was not speaking of normal hunger. But it appeared that the Duke's mistress was impossible to insult. In response, she laughed out loud. It was all the more annoying that there was nothing ribald about the sound. Her laugh was as pretty as the rest of her.

Abby hurried on, up the stairs and to her room, trying not to think about the activities that might have caused the Marchioness to be so hungry. It was obviously something more than a single kiss. For her part, even the simple breakfast she'd taken had sat on the plate uneaten, as her mind replayed her visit to Danforth's bedroom.

As she picked up the sewing basket, she vowed that, starting from this moment on, she would not let the man affect her so. She would deliver the silk to her mother, then go back to the breakfast room for another cup of tea. If Lenore was still present, she would converse with her as if she'd seen nothing unusual in her activities this morning. And if the Duke was there...

She rather hoped he wasn't. But if he was, she'd give him the same polite uninterest he usually gave to her. Perhaps, today, the rain would end. They might be on their way again tomorrow and she would never see him again.

She was headed back towards the stairs when she heard a quiet sob from the hall to her left and an emphatic shushing in response.

Abby paused before the corner, hoping that, if she allowed them a moment, the person or persons in distress might return to their room before they were discovered.

Instead, the initial sob was followed by feminine weeping and a familiar male voice ordering her, 'For pity's sake, be quiet if you don't want to attract the attention of the whole house.'

This was followed by a loud sniff and a shuddering, 'Yes, Your Grace.'

Abby froze in her tracks, just a few feet shy of the corner.

On the night before her wedding, she had received a

graphic description of what she could expect from the Duke once they were in the bedchamber. Her mother had assured her that, no matter what might occur, Danforth would be sensible of her inexperience and treat her with care. But her mother had been wrong. It seemed he was the sort of man to bother a woman in a common hallway.

Even when her opinion of him had been at its lowest, she had not imagined that. Even worse, the woman being accosted could not be Lady Beverly, who was already downstairs. Abby doubted that woman had ever shed a tear in her life. Even if she had, it would be the stuff of Minerva novels, a droplet of crystal and not the eye-reddening, dripping and sniffing variety that mere mortals wept.

It was not precisely a surprise to think that he would be false to his mistress and his fiancée at the same time. She had but to consider her own father to know that some men were inherently faithless and there was little to be done about it. Since she had just decided not to trouble herself over the behaviour of the Duke and his mistress, the sensible thing to do was to turn and walk quickly back to her room. She could wait there for a few minutes until the hall was empty. She shook her head in disgust and turned to go, until his next words stopped her.

'Be a good girl and be quiet. If you let me finish without making another peep, I will give you half a crown and we will never speak of this again.'

He was bothering a maid. She was aware that men sometimes took advantage of women in their employ.

But no true gentlemen would do such a thing. It was even worse that it should be a servant of a supposed friend and he would attempt something here where anyone might see, bribing his victim to silence while he took his pleasure.

The whole situation turned her empty stomach. She had been a fool to feel the least bit charitable towards him, sighing into her pillow about his kiss. He was a villain. There could be no more polite silence between them. Since it was clear that there was no one else to rescue this poor girl, she would do it herself and mince no words when telling Danforth what she thought of him.

She charged around the corner to surprise the pair of them, with a, 'Now see, here…', only to stumble over the back of the Duke who was on all fours in the middle of the floor. She landed, half on him, half over him, palms on the rug and slippers kicking in the air.

'And now I shall have to start over.' He shot a glance over his shoulder and gave her a baleful look before tipping her off on to the floor. Then, he looked back to the rug and muttered, 'Mind where you step when you get up. If you are not careful, you will crush some of them.'

'Crush what?' she said, scrambling to her feet, too curious to rebuke him.

'Lady Sanderson's pearls.' Abby turned to look for the speaker and saw a maid in the doorway next to them, her cheeks red and her face still wet with tears. 'My lady broke the string and I was going to see if Lady Elmstead's maid might have some silk. But His Grace was walking down the hallway…'

'Bumped right into her,' he muttered without looking up. 'Beads everywhere. We are still one short.' He glanced up at Abby, clearly annoyed. 'Or were, until a moment ago.' Then he plucked a pearl out of the rug and stuffed it into the handkerchief bundled in his left hand.

'Let me help.' Abby dropped to her knees, taking care that nothing was trapped beneath her skirts as she did so. It took only a moment for her to find a handful of loose pearls and point out the final one stuck in a crack in the baseboard, a place too tiny for her fingers to reach.

Without asking permission, the Duke pulled a pin from her hair and stabbed at the last pearl until it rolled free, then opened the bundle, added it and poked gingerly at the pile, counting under his breath. Then he twisted the linen again and offered it to the maid. 'Here you are. All thirty, safe and sound.' She took the pearls and was about to run off when he held a finger in the air to indicate she wait. Then he fished in his pocket and pulled out the coin he had promised, tossing it to her. 'In the future, watch where you are going.'

'Yes, Your Grace.'

When the maid had departed, he rolled to sit with his back against the wall and gave Abby a searching look. 'Thank you for your help, Miss Prescott.'

'Sometimes, a fresh set of eyes are needed,' she said with a shrug, getting to her feet and smoothing her skirt. 'It was kind of you to come to the girl's aid.'

'It was my fault,' he said, with a shrug. 'If I had not been distracted with my own thoughts, I would have been able to avoid running into her and would not have caused such a problem.'

He was looking at her as though she was somehow at fault as well. It made her…not precisely uncomfortable. But as she stared back into his very green eyes, it felt as if no time had passed since he'd put her out of his room on the previous evening. She wet her lips and tried to keep her mind on the conversation they were having. 'A broken necklace is hardly a problem.'

'Not to you, perhaps. But if the girl had found twenty-nine pearls instead of thirty, Lady Sanderson would have noticed. She broke the necklace by toying with the thing obsessively and likely knows the number of the beads better than the names of her own children.'

Abby nodded. She had been seated next to the woman at dinner and had been annoyed by the continual tick-ticking of the strand twisting and untwisting right next to her ear.

He continued. 'She is also the sort who believes the worst in people, especially those in her employ. She will count them once they have been repaired, assuming that her maid would have taken the opportunity to pocket one.'

'She'd have sacked the girl for the loss,' Abby said, surprised not to have realised the fact herself.

'When I bumped into her and she lost the loose beads, she burst into tears. It was clear that the poor thing was terrified. Unjustly so, for I have seen the care she takes with her employer's toilette.'

Abby nodded. While all the ladies at the party were

exceptionally well turned out, Lady Sanderson was never less than perfect, from dawn to midnight.

'I did what I could to help,' the Duke said absently.

'Not everyone would have,' she said, still slightly amazed. She had thought him distant because he did not speak and so exalted that he was unaware of the people around him. But it was clear that he watched constantly and was concerned for everyone, even those that she had assumed would be far beneath his notice.

'I am not just anyone, Miss Prescott.' To belie his words, the corner of his mouth twitched up into a self-deprecating smile.

'Of course not, Your Grace,' she replied, not totally sure if she was allowed to share in the joke.

'So formal? I would think, after last night, you would be entitled to call me Benedict.'

'Benedict,' she repeated and felt her plan to remain cool to him slipping away like smoke.

'Last night,' he repeated, savouring the memory for a moment. Then his smile changed to something much more pensive. 'I did not take the time to properly apologise for what happened.'

He was sorry.

She let out the breath she had been holding, not sure if she was relieved or disappointed. 'That is not necessary. It was a simple misunderstanding.'

'On the contrary. It was very forward of me to take a kiss without asking your leave,' he said.

'Do not think about it,' she said, unable to tear her gaze away from his lips. She could remember the feel of them, remember the taste. Suddenly, she was hungry for more.

There was something shy in his manner, as if he had honestly believed she would have refused him if he asked again. But though she reminded herself that nothing had happened to change her opinion about their unsuitability, it would be much harder to say no if he offered another kiss.

He shifted until he was on his knees and held out his hand to her and she took it, ready to help him from the floor. But she did not feel the tug that indicated he was about to rise. Instead, he remained there, kneeling at her feet, his hand in hers. 'I do not want to forget our kiss. In fact, I have been able to think of little else.'

His hand was warm in hers and, before she could stop herself, she gave it a squeeze of encouragement.

He made no attempt to respond. 'Making assumptions about your desires has led me into no end of trouble, thus far. I thought it might be possible to undo the damage I did during our engagement. But I would hate to think that I have already spoiled my chances with precipitous action.'

They had far more to discuss than his tendency to act without speaking. But she would never be able to make him understand her difficulties if she did not give him a chance to know her better. Would that knowledge include more kissing? He had declared it unforgettable. She had not known how much she had wanted to hear the words until he had spoken them. But he had also apologised.

He was staring at her as if some sort of answer

was required, but she was still not sure what she was supposed to say. If there was a chance to rewrite the history between them and come to an honest understanding, then she most certainly wanted to try.

She nodded.

But before she could do more, there was an excited gasp from the stairs behind them. Her mother was hurrying up the last few steps towards them, Mrs Eames and Mrs Crompton just a step behind. 'Oh, my dear, I had no idea things were progressing so quickly.'

Abby felt the sharp tug on her arm that she had expected earlier, as the Duke pulled himself to his feet, turning to greet the ladies with a look of horror on his face.

In response, her mother waved her hands in refusal, and curtsied. 'Please, do not let us interrupt, Your Grace.' She giggled. 'Or should I say, my son?'

Chapter Eight

'Please, Mother, just stop talking.'

'But what else could he have meant by such behaviour?' her mother asked, loud enough to be heard by the guests in the sitting room. 'Danforth was kneeling at your feet and holding your hand.'

Mrs Eames and Mrs Crompton nodded in agreement. Heads appeared in doorways up and down the main hall, then disappeared again, once they had ascertained who was speaking.

'It was not at all as it appeared,' Abby replied, in a voice loud enough to carry through to the main floor.

'Well, what was it, then?' her mother asked.

There was a feeling of tension in the air, as if the whole house held its breath, awaiting her answer.

The logical thing to do would be to tell the truth. But since Danforth had gone out of his way to conceal it for the sake of the maid, she did not think he would want her to announce it to everyone within earshot. She had to think of something better.

But why should it be her responsibility at all? He could have helped explain away the mess he had helped to cause. Instead, it had taken him only an instant to regain his composure. Then he had smiled at the ladies staring at them, wished them a good morning and strolled to his room as if nothing had happened, abandoning her to make this explanation on her own.

Her mother's interrogation was enough to set her teeth on edge. But the fact that there was an audience hiding in the rooms all around them was unbearable. She had to say something, anything at all, that would make it possible to escape. 'He was inebriated,' she blurted, offering a silent prayer for forgiveness of this enormous lie.

'In the middle of the day?' her mother said, surprised.

'I suspect so,' Abby allowed, hoping her doubt would give the Duke some chance to come up with a better story, later. 'When I came back from getting the silk, I found him sitting on the floor in the hallway. I was trying to get him on his feet when you arrived.'

'Men are sometimes more free with their words when they are in their cups,' her mother replied. 'Did he say anything to you?'

'Nothing of importance,' Abby said, casting a worried glance towards the sitting room.

'Because he was looking at you most fondly, just now,' her mother said. 'And Miss Sommersby has told everyone that he was holding your hand last night in the card room.'

'Miss Sommersby was mistaken,' she said hurriedly.

'Are you sure there was no hint…?'

What was the true answer to that? She wanted there to be something. But not as much as her mother did. And certainly not as much as a house full of bored guests who were hanging on every word, every glance, every shared joke. If there was nothing to find, they would make something up.

She gave her mother a firm smile. 'Nothing, Mama. He was in need of aid and I helped him. That is all.'

Her mother sighed. 'What a pity. And a pity about his drinking as well. He will not keep his handsome looks for long if he cannot keep out of the brandy bottle until after supper.'

'That is no business of ours, Mama,' she said, pushing her sewing basket, complete with red silk, into her mother's arms. 'Now let us go back to our needlework and mind our business.'

It seemed rather weak-willed for a grown man to hide in his bedroom to avoid gossip. But for the moment, it was the only solution Benedict had come up with. At the sight of Mrs Prescott and her friends, he had released Abigail as quickly as possible, made his apologies and disappeared without explanation.

If he had thought the incident would die without comment, he had been a fool. It had taken less than an hour before a knock sounded on the door of the Tudor room. The sound was masculine in its decisiveness, as if delivered by someone who required an explanation and would demand it, if it was not given freely, post-haste.

He put down the book he had been reading. 'Come in, Comstock.'

If the Earl was surprised by his correct guess, he showed no sign of the fact as he entered. 'I am sorry to disturb you, Your Grace, but I was given to understand that you might be in some distress.'

'I?' he said, surprised. If anyone needed consolation, he'd have expected it to be Abigail.

For the briefest of moments, Comstock seemed to be stifling a smile. Then, his expression returned to one of gentlemanly concern. 'Yes. There was talk among the guests that you might not be able to see a hole in a ladder.'

'I beg your pardon?'

Comstock cleared his throat. 'That you might be a trifle disguised.' When Benedict did not immediately respond, he added, 'Bosky. Foxed. Drunk as a wheelbarrow and crawling down the upper halls on your hands and knees, unable to rise without help.'

'Inebriated?' he said in a tone meant to wipe the smile off the Earl's face, for he was close to laughing at Benedict's expense. 'Whatever gave you that idea?'

'That is Miss Prescott's story,' the Earl said, his smile turning sympathetic. 'Her mother is under the impression that she interrupted a proposal. But Miss Abigail insists that it was nothing of the kind and that she was only trying to help you to your feet.'

'I see,' Benedict replied, making sure that his voice was as sober as his expression.

The Earl continued. 'The rest of the household is split on which they think is the most likely answer.

But each side is supporting their theory with clandestine meetings they claim to have witnessed or times when they suspected that your cologne masked the scent of gin.'

He had chosen wrong. He should have followed the Prescotts down the stairs from the first. His presence would have stifled the gossip before it began. Then, Abigail would not have had to come up with a story to preserve her reputation. 'And which side are you on?'

'I think the explanation is obvious enough,' Comstock replied. 'When I saw her just now, Miss Prescott's hair was falling down as if she had just been tussling with someone. A short time before that, you were caught by her mother, down on one knee…'

'Both knees,' Benedict insisted. 'And just a single curl was out of place. I needed to borrow a hairpin.'

Comstock's expression now said he could not quite believe what he was hearing. 'Were you picking locks? If a door is shut, you need only ask me and I will give you a key.'

'Do not be ridiculous,' Benedict snapped. 'There is a perfectly logical explanation. If you could manage to stop laughing at me for a moment and listen.' But the further he got in the story, the more irrational his behaviour sounded.

By the time he had finished, Comstock's smile had become a sceptical grimace. 'An impromptu engagement makes far more sense than what you just told me.'

'Perhaps it does. But Miss Prescott and I are nowhere near to that. We have only just begun to speak again.'

The Earl gave a nod of approval, then frowned. 'You could not converse standing up?'

'I was apologising,' Benedict admitted. 'For kissing her.'

'Hmm.' By the look on Comstock's face, he was imagining the sort of situation that would require such an apology and wondering if the lady needed rescuing from an unwelcome advance.

'It was an honest mistake,' Benedict added, remembering why it was that he did not like conversing with strangers. It seldom seemed to go the way he expected. 'I doubt it will happen again. If the whole house suspects that there is something between us, they shall be watching our every move, trying to catch us together.' And that was not what he had wanted at all. 'I doubt we will have another moment's privacy for the rest of the week.'

'Do you wish for one?' Comstock asked. 'More importantly, does the lady wish to be alone with you again?'

'I do,' Benedict replied, relieved. 'And I do not think Miss Prescott would object to it, should the opportunity present itself.'

Comstock gave a sigh of relief. 'If all you require is privacy, you shall have it. As I have told you before, this is a very large house.' He thought for a moment. 'And what do you wish me to do about the rumours currently circulating about the pair of you?'

'Ignore them. That is what I plan to do.' People only had to look at him to know he was not a drunkard. And as for his re-engagement to Abigail Prescott?

That might be true, soon enough. 'As long as people do not learn the truth of us before I am ready to tell it, I do not care what stories they make up for themselves.'

'If that is what you wish, Your Grace.' Comstock's words were agreeable enough, but the look in his eyes said that he saw trouble ahead.

When he came down to the salon before supper, it was clear that, after finding herself at the centre of several fresh rumours, Miss Prescott was going out of her way to avoid further gossip. She made a point of staying on the far side of the room from him, moving away each time he tried to come close to her. During the meal, her mother seemed even chattier than usual. But Abigail kept her eyes on her plate and made little effort to speak to the ladies on either side of her, chewing and swallowing methodically as if the excellent food had no flavour at all.

Later, when the men joined the ladies in the parlour, she made sure that the seats at her card table were always occupied so there would be no chance of receiving another of the Danforth family heirlooms. When the game ended, she shared a sofa with her mother, so deep in conversation that there was no hope of interrupting.

Since it was clear that there was to be no romantic tête-à-tête or shared smiles to support a clandestine engagement, the party began to look for proof of the other rumour. Each time his glass was refilled he felt rather than heard a collective intake of breath, as the room monitored him for signs of unsteadiness. Unable to resist, he tossed the last of his drink back with obvious relish and grinned at them.

From her usual place at his side, Lenore laughed.

'Drowning your sorrows, Danforth?'

'Giving the people what they want,' he said.

'Bread and circuses?' she asked.

He nodded.

'Then let me play.' She whispered the last words into his ear.

He knew what would come next. It was a trick they'd played often enough when one or the other of them had wanted to escape a party, leaving no question of where they were going. It was effective. But tonight, he wished there were some other way.

Lenore was staring across the room, her gaze fixed on the place where the Prescotts sat. It lingered there until Abigail felt it and looked in their direction. Then his friend turned back to look up at him, tracing a fingertip along the shoulder of his coat before yawning dramatically and wishing him a goodnight.

As he had done so many times before, he waited twenty minutes before bidding his own goodnights to the group and following Lenore up the stairs.

Chapter Nine

Abby waited a full hour after Danforth retired before she deemed it safe to go to her room. If she wanted to maintain the illusion that there was nothing between her and the Duke, she must act as if she believed it herself.

All the other women in the room did not care about him in any but the most academic way. He was a curiosity to be observed. His relationship with his mistress even more so. It did not hurt any of the other ladies to see them together. Their mouths did not go dry when the Marchioness whispered in his ear, nor did they feel their own skin burn as those delicate fingers brushed the wool of his coat. When Lady Beverly left the room after one long, lingering glance in his direction, the people around her hid their smiles, trying to pretend that they did not understand what they were seeing.

But Abby knew and so did Danforth. He poured another drink, glanced in her direction and held it up in toast before finishing it in a gulp. Then he waited. More accurately, he pretended to. In less than a half an hour, he excused himself. Once the door had closed behind him, the room buzzed with whispered comments and knowing chuckles.

And, just as she'd known there would be had she married him, there were looks cast in her direction. Pitying, knowing and equally curious. They were wondering if she understood. She was a good daughter who had been raised to be a good wife, so she did what was expected of her and pretended that she had no idea what was happening upstairs, at this very moment.

But she did know and the truth felt like ants, crawling on her skin. She reached for a shawl to hide her trembling and made an offhand comment about a chill. In truth, the room felt uncomfortably warm. She forced herself to make polite conversation with her mother for a few minutes, then moved back to one of the card tables and laid out game after game of patience, though she was too distracted to know or care about the figures on the cards in front of her. She watched as Lady Elmstead retired and then the Sandersons.

When at least an hour had passed since the Duke's departure, she put aside the cards and announced herself ready for bed. Then she progressed towards her room at a leisurely pace, giving no indication to the people left in the room that she had even noticed the Duke's absence.

When she arrived at her bedroom door, the black-and-white dog was already waiting for her. He looked up at her and stomped his little feet, then gave an expectant huff before trotting a few feet down the hall.

When she did not immediately follow, he trotted back to her, staring up.

She looked down at him with a sigh. 'Must we do this again tonight?'

The dog eyed her shoe for a moment as if considering, then laid a single, warning paw on the diamante clip decorating it. Then he looked down the hall in the direction of the unoccupied rooms.

'Very well, then. If we can dispense with the thievery, that is something, at least. Lead on, MacDuff.'

Tonight, the dog took her further down the back hallway to an open door. She stood on the doorstep, looking into a candlelit bedroom where the Duke of Danforth lounged on a dusty coverlet. He looked up at her, making no effort to rise. 'I thought you would never get here.'

She stared directly at him, resisting the urge to search the corners of the room for some sign that Lady Beverly had been and gone. 'I thought you had better things to do at this hour than to bother me.'

He laughed. 'And what might they be?'

As usual, he was forcing her to admit to knowledge she never should have had. 'Spending time with your friend Lenore.' Though she gritted her teeth to prevent them, the words forced themselves out of her.

'If I meant to be with her this evening, I would still be there,' he said, his laughter changing to a soft, sympathetic smile. 'Although, it is often said that drunkards lack the stamina to perform the acts you are imagining.'

She swallowed nervously, for she had forgotten what she had accused him of, earlier in the day.

'You told everyone I was a drunkard,' he reminded her, shaking his head in amazement.

'I am sorry,' she blurted, her anger turning to embarrassment. Then she gripped the door frame, waiting for the explosion she was sure would come.

'Cringing? I did not expect that from you.' His voice held the faintly flat tone she had heard in London as he'd proposed. It was not precisely emotionless, just far too measured to be appropriate for the occasion.

She did not realise she had closed her eyes against his anger until she had to open one of them to gauge his true mood.

He was still smiling at her in a polite, distant way that was suitable for a drawing room or a ball. When he was sure she could see it, he crooked his finger, beckoning her into the room. 'Come closer. I do not bite.' She took a step forward and he added, 'At least, not in such a way as you'd mind.'

She stopped.

He let out an exasperated sigh. In a flickering of candlelight, he seemed to relax, transforming from the distant and sophisticated peer into someone much more human. And then he was gone again and the noble had returned. 'Really, I thought you were made of sterner stuff than this.'

Other than standing up to him, she could not think of where he had got such an idea.

'Come on, then, and close the door behind you. We must talk and I will not have that little dog listening to us as we do. I fear he will relay the conversation to his owner.'

'Dogs don't talk,' she scoffed, before realising that he was joking. His face and voice gave her none of the clues that she would have looked for to tell her so.

'Of course, they don't. But in this house, I would not be surprised to find the exception. For all his rough, country manners, Comstock is wickedly smart and his wife is just the same.'

'I see,' she said, still totally confused, remaining on the doorstep.

He crooked his finger again. 'Never mind the dog. We must still discuss the Banbury tale that you told to the other guests this afternoon.'

'I am terribly sorry to have defamed you in that way, Your Grace. I will explain tomorrow that I was obviously mistaken,' she said, inching towards the hallway. 'And now, if you will excuse me, I think we've spent enough time alone together for the day.'

Before she could complete her retreat, he'd sprung from the bed and moved behind her, closing the door on a yip of disapproval from the terrier. 'It is no longer day,' he said. He was now standing so close that she could feel his breath on the back of her neck, which made her spin to face him and back further into the room, just as he'd intended. 'It has been night for some time and is very near to being tomorrow.'

She swallowed again. 'I do not plan to remain with you until morning, if that is what you are suggesting.'

He arched an eyebrow. 'Actually, that had not occurred to me. But I find it interesting that your mind runs so quickly in that direction,' he said. 'It likely explains why your body runs in the opposite way, each time I try to get close to you.' Then he smiled. It was one of his rare, true smiles, the sort that made his eyes crinkle at the corners.

'I am not running,' she said, dragging her gaze from the kissable dimple that had appeared in his left cheek. She lifted her chin and tried to show some of the strength of character that he seemed to think she had. 'I am simply trying to maintain a respectful distance.'

'Respect for whom?' he asked. 'If it is for me, you needn't bother. A title does not mean I need to be treated like a glass ornament and observed from a distance. And if it is respect for you?' He smiled again in a way that was magnetically attractive, and yet quite frightening. 'I give you my word that you are perfectly safe, both in person and reputation. Nothing will happen between us that you do not agree to.'

If that had been meant to give reassurance, it failed utterly. If the previous evening had taught her anything, it was that she was likely to agree to do things with him that were not the least bit wise. 'Since you are still blocking the doorway, I find it difficult to believe you.'

He held his hands in the air palms forward, in surrender, and walked towards her, circling her as she returned to her position near the now-closed door. The distance between them remained the same, like a carefully choreographed dance where the partners could be connected without needing to touch. 'Better?'

She gave him a hesitant nod. She was able to escape again, should she need to. But as she had the previous night, she felt a strange sense of disappointment. 'I am simply trying to avoid any more awkward situations that might lead to gossip.'

'That has already been taken care of, for this evening, at least.'

She frowned. 'What do you mean?'

'You cannot lie and claim you did not notice the show Lenore put on, since you already remarked on it.'

'It was in show?' she said, still doubtful.

'She made sure that, whatever people assumed you and I were doing after we left the drawing room, they would not assume that we were together,' he said. Now his eyes had a suggestive twinkle that made her eager, but uneasy.

'To what end?' she said, confused.

'I will not speak for Lenore. It is none of my business what she is up to or where she spends her nights. But I wished to talk with you.'

'What do you want with me?' she asked. Perhaps it was the shape of the room that made her voice sound so desperate for his attention. She cleared her throat and tried again. 'What did you wish to talk about?'

'Your lie?' he said, with an inclination of his head to remind her that he had already told her. When she opened her mouth for a second, more fervent apology, he cut her off. 'I wished for you to know that it does not matter to me in the slightest what story you told. You needed to say something to explain the scene in the hall. I am more than content to take the blame for the incident, if it spares your reputation and the position of the silly girl that caused the problem in the first place.'

'But now people will think you are an inebriate,' she reminded him.

'For a week or so, perhaps,' he allowed. 'They will watch me closely and sniff discreetly at my breath and my clothing. And then they will remember that I am, on the whole, a temperate man and they will lose interest and go bother someone else.'

His response was so different from the way her father might have reacted that, at first, she could hardly be sure she had heard it correctly.

He must have noticed her confusion, for he added, 'You look surprised.'

'I was prepared for a much more volatile response,' she admitted.

'Would my shouting at you have helped in any way?' he asked.

'No,' she admitted.

He nodded, as if that settled the matter. 'It is not my way to make you march through the halls in a hair shirt, weeping and beating your breast in penance for the way you have treated me, in the past or present.'

He was speaking of the wedding again. 'I should not have left you in the church with no explanation,' she admitted.

'Then why did you?' he asked. There was no malice in his voice, only a gentle curiosity. 'I can understand why you did not want to marry me. I admit that I did not give you time to consider my proposal or reason to accept. But why did you not simply tell me that you needed more time to consider my offer?'

It was a painfully logical question. But as the date

had approached, she had not been so clear-headed as the Duke had been. 'I was angry,' she whispered, for her anger was the easiest emotion to explain.

'At me?' he said, as oblivious as ever.

'The week before the wedding, I went with my mother to Bond Street, to have the final fitting for my wedding gown.'

'I saw you in the window of the shop. You were standing in the light from the street, trying to choose a trim.' His smile of remembrance was fond and a little proud as if her appearance and behaviour had somehow reflected upon him. It was further proof that he did not understand the problem at all.

'You were not alone,' she reminded him, still amazed that he did not see what was wrong. 'Lady Beverly was there, as well.'

'We were shopping together,' he admitted.

'You were laughing,' she said. 'At me.'

'Not at you.' He seemed surprised that she would even think such a thing.

'How was I to know?' she said, frustrated. 'You were staring directly at me, laughing and talking.'

'We were,' he agreed cautiously. 'I was pointing you out to Lenore. You seemed busy. I did not know you were aware of us.'

Not aware? When she had returned home, the embarrassment of that near meeting had left her retching into the chamber pot and unable to take a meal for the rest of the day. 'I pretended not to notice because it would not have been proper to acknowledge you,' she said, exasperated.

'Why ever not?' he said, still confused.

'Because you are not supposed to introduce your wife to your mistress,' she snapped. 'You are not supposed to flaunt your lover in my... I mean, in your wife's face. You certainly aren't supposed to bring her to house parties and then sneak upstairs to be with her...' Now that she had started, she could not seem to stop talking. The rage that she had felt since the day she'd seen them watching her on Bond Street came pouring out, leaving her embarrassingly close to tears.

'As I told you before, that was a ruse to make it possible for us to be together, unsuspected.'

'You did not tell me that until after,' she snapped. 'You abandoned me in the sitting room, where everyone was gossiping about the pair of you.'

'I suspect so,' he said. 'But since I never listen to gossip, it does not bother me.'

'But it bothers me to have to hear it. I can tell that they are wondering what I think of it and pitying me for being engaged to a man who would treat me with so little regard. And the minute I left, I am sure that those remaining in the room discussed the matter aloud and at length.' The chill she had felt in the sitting room was returning. She felt alone and vulnerable, fully clothed and yet exposed.

But as usual, the Duke appeared to be unmoved. He waited patiently until her words stopped, leaving only the sound of her ragged breathing in the quiet of the room. Then he stepped forward, taking her cold hand and stroking the back of it with his thumb as if trying to calm her. 'You needn't worry,' he said, at last.

'None of what they say about us is true, because she is not my mistress.'

Though she was still close to tears, she laughed, for it was the most ridiculous excuse he could have given for his behaviour. 'So she told me. But everyone knows that the two of you are intimate.' Her throat closed again, as she thought of the way Lenore had caressed him and the smile full of promise she had given him before she had left the room.

'Then what everyone knows is wrong,' he said. 'We are well aware of what people think. But I have never claimed a romantic relationship with her. It is just as well that people do not dare to ask me about it.' He smiled. 'I have never had to lie. This evening, she employed a trick that we have often used when we wish privacy. There are people downstairs right now discussing what they assume I am doing. But they will never guess the truth.'

Instead, they thought something far worse. 'Why would you do such a thing?' she said.

'If everyone thinks I am with her, your honour is safe. No one will be thinking about you,' he said. 'No one, except me, of course.' His smile grew much warmer and she felt her reservations begin to melt.

'Your former paramour is encouraging you to be alone with me,' she said, shaking her head to clear her mind of the romantic fog developing in it.

'My friend,' he corrected. 'You needn't be concerned about her jealousy because she feels none.'

'I do not care about her feelings,' Abby said, tugging her hand from his grasp. 'Just as I was on the day of our wedding, I am more concerned with what will happen to me when you grow bored with the novelty of having a wife and return to her.'

'You still do not understand,' he said, reaching for her again. 'She is not my lover now, she was not my lover in the past and she will not be my lover in the future.'

'Not ever?' she asked.

'Never,' he said. His voice had gone flat again and his smile had returned to its former, bland politeness. But when she looked more closely, she could see the slight crease of his brow and the drawn brows that passed for anger in the emotionless Duke of Danforth.

'Everyone knows about you,' she said.

'Truth is not defined by what everyone knows,' he said.

She nodded. 'Truth is normally defined by facts. The facts are that you and Lady Beverly have been virtually inseparable since her husband's death. When you are seen together, you keep an intimate distance from each other, whispering and sharing jokes. You laugh and talk freely, just as you did that day on Bond Street. And though you meant to spend the rest of your life with me, you did not bother to tell me this alleged truth until now. What do you have to prove the innocence of your relationship, against the preponderance of evidence?'

'Only my word,' he said, in a voice filled with warning.

'Men are quick to evoke that when they speak to each other,' she said. 'But it seldom keeps them from lying to women.'

'Then the first thing you must know about me is that I would not use that phrase lightly to a man or a woman. You have my word that I have never lain with Lenore.' And this time, his voice was undeniably sincere and his face held no trace of a smile.

'There has never been anything between you?' she said, eyes narrowed.

He paused. There was a world of meaning in that brief silence.

'And now I know what your word is good for,' she said, turning to go.

'I proposed to her. Once. I was seventeen at the time. She refused. It is fortunate that she did for it would have been a horrible mistake for us to marry. We truly do not suit. But none of this is common knowledge and has been a secret between the two of us since the day it happened.'

This was even more puzzling. A youthful mistake was the sort of detail that many people might omit from a story without technically lying. But it had been enough to make Danforth hesitate when she'd questioned him. It was also more information than she had expected him to share about any part of his life, before or after they were married. 'If what you say is true...' She held up a hand to keep him from interrupting. 'Then what is the reason for secrecy? Why have you cultivated this illusion for nearly a decade? Why not simply tell people the truth?'

Now he hesitated, as if the easiest answer was the lie that he refused to tell. At last he said, 'My reason is my friendship for Lenore. And her reason is something

I cannot share with you, since the facts were given to me in confidence. If she chooses to release me, then I will tell you all. But until that time, I swear on my honour that when I offered for you, you had no rival for my attention, nor would there have been one after we had married.'

This time, when he reached for her, he took both hands. His grip was gentle, open so she might pull free if she wished. He held just the tips of her fingers, cupped in his, thumbs resting lightly on top. 'I am sorry that our behaviour this evening upset you and that you had to suffer the scrutiny of the other guests because of it. But tonight, I wanted to be alone with you.'

'Then here I am,' she said. 'What do you want from me?'

'I want to know you better.' He smiled and his fingers tightened almost imperceptibly. 'And I want you to know me. That will take time.'

He was raising hopes in her, just as it had in the hall when he'd been kneeling at her feet. Then she remembered that, even if she was not his mistress, Lady Beverly was just down the hall, eager to hear the results of this meeting. Her mother was here, too, and she had already seen too much disappointment on their account. 'Perhaps, when we are back in London…'

He tugged on her hands, pulling her forward. His arms were circling her and his lips were close to her ear. 'Why must we wait?' Then, he kissed her. It was different from the last kiss, which had been passionate, but rushed. Tonight, he took his time, tasting first

the top lip, then, the bottom, holding them gently between his and stroking them with his tongue. Then he
pressed his open mouth to hers and she felt him smile.

If she yielded tonight, she would not be able to claim
that she had acted foolishly, in the heat of the moment. He was giving her time to remember the dozen
reasons why she should push him away and run back
to her room. But though she might wish for a better
time, a better place, what if this opportunity never
came again?

Hesitantly, she wrapped her arms around his waist
and touched the tip of her tongue to his. Last night, the
feeling had come upon her in a rush and had passed just
as suddenly. But tonight, it was a slow-growing surety.
First, she wanted him to kiss her. Then she wanted as
much as he wanted to take from her.

He was teasing her, his tongue darting in and out of
her mouth, gone almost as soon as it arrived. His hands
moved on her back, fingers spread, sliding upwards to
reach the skin above her gown. Then his tongue moved
with more urgency, as she felt him undoing the hooks
of her bodice and the silk slipping down her arms,
leaving her shoulders bare.

He pulled away with a sigh and rained kisses down
her jaw, down her throat, burying his face at the base of
her neck to inhale her cologne before kissing the top of
her shoulder. 'You smell of springtime,' he whispered.

And he smelled of spice and sin. There was nothing innocent about the fragrance that enveloped her.
It made her legs tremble, eager to spread. One of his
hands had moved to her breast, pushing down her stays

and cupping it through the light fabric of her chemise. His fingers circled her nipple, then pinched, making her gasp.

'May I kiss you here?' he said, giving another little tug. 'Or would you prefer that we wait until we are back in London?'

'Villain,' she whispered.

'If that is what you think, I shall behave accordingly,' he said and his mouth closed on her breast.

The sensation was exquisite, hot and cold at the same time as his head moved from one to the other. Then he stopped to look up at her. 'What do you think of my villainy now?' he asked, brushing her nipples with his fingertips.

A curious sensation had taken the place of the nervous tension she'd felt in the sitting room. She still wanted to shiver, but the feelings came from inside her skin, not on it. 'This is not proper,' she said, when she could manage to form words.

'This is a trifle compared to what I want from you,' he said, pausing to nibble on her collarbone. 'And what I would have taken had I been given the chance in London.'

'Taken?' she said, shocked.

'I had no right to kiss you, until we were properly wed,' he said, staring down at her breasts in fascination. 'But I wanted so much more. If it were up to me, I'd have pulled you from the dance floor on the first night and laid you bare until I had looked my fill.'

'That would have been wrong,' she whispered, shocked at how right it sounded.

'Then I suppose it would have been wrong if I'd leaned you against the mantelpiece in your parents' parlour and taken you hard, the minute I'd put my ring on your finger,' he said.

'You would not have done so,' she said, trying to remember the stiff and proper gentleman who had barely looked at her when he'd proposed.

He was toying with her breasts again, one in each hand as he murmured against her throat. 'I would have. Until you screamed with pleasure. And then I'd have dragged you back to my own bed for the three weeks until the wedding.'

The strange feelings inside her were growing stronger, centring deep within her. 'Why would I stay in bed for so long?' she said, trying to catch her breath.

'Because between sleeping, I would be on you, under you and in you,' he said. 'You would be too weak from pleasure to stand. I would be doing unspeakable things to you and you would beg me for more.' Then his head dropped again and he nipped her breast.

At the touch of his teeth, the nerves in her body hummed like violin strings. As the bite became a kiss, they tightened, vibrating, thrumming and throbbing, the feeling growing and joining until they combined in a chord, shaking her to the core, leaving her panting, wet and willing.

His hands moved to her bottom, giving a lazy squeeze as his mouth released her nipple and he looked into her eyes. His smile widened. 'Did you peak?' he said, searching her face. 'From a few kisses and the sound of my voice?' He seemed to have found whatever he was searching for, for he spoke his next words in an awed whisper. 'I believe you did.'

She looked away, embarrassed. 'I don't know what you mean.' At least, she was not sure she did. But she suspected that it had something to do with the way she felt as he'd kissed her. But if it was something that was only supposed to occur during the marital act, it was possible that she had done something wrong.

He touched her chin with a fingertip, forcing her to look into his eyes. 'If the bedding in this room weren't so dusty, I would teach you right now.'

The suggestion brought another wave of delight, as if the very centre of her longed for him to take her. But she would be a fool to give herself with no guarantee of a future. 'You should not say such things,' she said, tugging her gown back up, trying and failing to make herself respectable.

He adjusted the bodice, then spun her around and did up the hooks. 'You are right. Even with a woman as delightfully responsive as you, it is much more pleasant to act than to talk.'

Compliments. She should be enjoying them. But even though her body cried out for the lessons he was offering, she knew that she needed more than pretty words before she did more. She had already learned the folly of pledging herself to a man she did not understand. It would be an even greater mistake to allow him liberties without such a pledge. 'We should not act, either,' she said. 'I think we have done far too much already.'

'You are probably right,' he said, whispering into

her ear. Then he sighed and gave her a gentle kiss on the back of the neck before turning her to face him again. 'You should return to your room now. Unaccompanied, of course. There are limits to the gullibility of any party, and we must not be seen together after they think we have retired.'

'Of course,' she said faintly. He knew far more about such things than she did. Young ladies were not supposed to have liaisons any more than they were supposed to associate with the mistresses of their husbands. But everyone in England knew that Danforth's love life existed on the brink of indiscretion. He did as he pleased and did not let the consequences concern him. If she stayed with him, she would have to live there with him.

He kissed her again, lightly, on the surprised 'O' of her mouth. Then, he stepped past her and opened the door, looking both ways to make sure there were no observers other than the black-and-white terrier who had waited for her. 'Until tomorrow, my dear Abigail.'

She nodded and stepped into the hall to follow the terrier back to her room.

Chapter Ten

'You are in a good mood this morning,' Lenore said, pouring his coffee for him as he filled his plate with eggs.

'No more so than usual,' he replied, trying not to smile. If the illusion they had created on the previous evening was to be maintained, Lenore should be the last person to be surprised that he was cheerful.

Now she raised her chin and gave a sniff, before sighing. '*L'amour.* It is in the air, is it not?'

He sniffed as well. 'I believe what you are smelling is the kippers. But suit yourself.'

She looked around the breakfast room to be sure that they would not be overheard. 'Truth, now. Did you meet with her? What happened?'

'We talked.' He should be embarrassed to admit that their conversation was the last thing on his mind this morning. He could still remember the taste of her lips and her sighs as she lost control.

The sound of a spoon clinking loudly against the side of a teacup brought him back to the present. Lenore ceased her unladylike stirring and grinned at him. 'You did far more than talk, I think. Will they be forced to read the banns, again? Or will it be special licence? I recommend the latter, so she has no chance to change her mind. It will also spare the rest of us from watching you behave like a mooncalf each time she is near.'

'When things progress to the point of a proposal, there will be no such problems,' he said, taking a sip of his coffee and trying to regain his composure. 'I do not intend to rush her this time. If I can get her to accept me, there will be nothing to frighten her or make her doubt my resolve.'

'Was that the problem last time?' Lenore leaned forward, eager to hear the details.

No. You were.

Many married men of his set kept mistresses. It had never occurred to him that appearing to have one would cause more trouble than having one. But, after last night, he hoped that matter was settled. After he'd told Abigail his part of the truth, she'd allowed him to kiss her. It had taken little more than that to have her close to fainting in his arms with desire. Surely, she must see that they belonged together. 'When we were in London, I should have reassured her of my intentions to respect her,' he said, then added, 'Of course, there is more to being a duchess than simply marrying a duke.'

'And what might that be?' By the look she was giving him, Lenore thought Abigail was making this courtship far more difficult than it needed to be.

'As my wife, she will undergo continual public scrutiny. People are always fascinated by the doings of their betters. The gossip that surrounds our friendship bothers her far too much.'

'She would be used to gossip by now, I should think,' Lenore said, staring over her teacup. 'Her parents cannot manage to leave the house without creating a scandal.'

'I had not noticed,' he said, buttering a slice of toast.

'Because you insist on ignoring things that happen right under your nose,' she replied.

'It has served me well, thus far,' he said, taking a sip of coffee. In his youth, he had allowed himself to be far too upset by mere words. The day he'd realised that his father never raised a hand to his family to accompany his ranting was the day that words had ceased to have any power over him.

'If you wish to understand Miss Prescott, you would benefit by paying attention to her family difficulties.'

'I would hardly call the fact that her mother married above herself to be a difficulty,' he said.

'How like a man to blame the wife,' Lenore replied, slathering marmalade on her bread. 'Though I suspect her daughter is sometimes disadvantaged by it, the fault does not lie in her mother's birth. Had she married any other man than that brute, Prescott, the *ton* would not find her nearly as annoying.'

'He is not with them, this trip,' Benedict remarked, not that he missed the man.

'Apparently, he has gone to Italy. There, he has been entertaining an opera singer with his wife's money.

You have not seen the hints in the scandal sheets about Mr. P. and La C.?'

'I have no time for such foolishness,' he reminded her.

'Not even when it pertains to someone you purport to care about,' Lenore said.

'Someone I do care about,' Benedict corrected, trying to ignore the niggling feelings of guilt at his negligence.

'It is probably fortunate for Miss Prescott that she jilted you,' Lenore replied. 'She has been rusticating in Somerset since the wedding. It gave her an excuse to avoid the scandal that her father created. As of late, when her mother accepts invitations, she knows she will be forced to endure the curiosity of people who read of her husband's betrayal in the papers each morning.' She paused, considering. 'Our antics are listed there as well. And, of course, the disaster that was your wedding. People are quite well versed in the history attached to Miss Prescott's parents. I can see why she might not want any more notoriety.'

'It can't have bothered her too much,' he said, trying to shake the feeling that he was somehow responsible for her unhappiness. 'Apparently, they were on their way back to town when the storm stopped them.'

'I had occasion to speak to Mrs Prescott the other night,' Lenore replied. 'She is not as obtuse as she appears. After the wedding, it was Miss Prescott's plan to leave town permanently and stick to her knitting. Her mother disagrees. Since John Prescott's profligacy is likely to grow worse rather than better, it is her opinion that Abigail must find a husband, before both fortune and youth are depleted. She will not do that by hiding in the country. When it was mentioned in the scandal sheets that you and I were away from town...'

'She hoped to make the most of my absence,' he said.

'The plan was to avoid gossip by avoiding you,' Lenore said, shaking her head. 'But that has been a dismal failure. And if the company here is any indication, society has not forgotten what she had done, nor is it likely to. The room buzzes with whispers each time she leaves the room. With you or without you, a scandal-free life in London will be nearly impossible for her.'

He had not noticed, since it was always silent when he was in a room. 'She is managing quite well, all things considered,' he supplied, trying not to think of her angry declaration of the night before.

'I suspect her mind is more at ease, now that you have explained our relationship,' Lenore said, then gave him a pointed look. 'You have explained, haven't you?'

'Do not treat me like an idiot child,' he said. 'I am perfectly able to handle Abigail Prescott.'

'That does not answer my question,' she said.

'I have explained as much as I am entitled to share,' he added, staring back at her.

If he had expected her to release him from his promise, he was disappointed. Instead she said, 'I will take care of the rest.'

'I would prefer that you left it to me,' he replied. 'As

you have reminded me, it should be up to me to make things right with Miss Prescott.'

'And I will make sure you have the time to do that,' she said, ignoring what he needed her to do. Then she yawned. 'Though we are not yet done with breakfast, I feel I will be in need of an afternoon nap. From a megrim, perhaps. I shall be in my room until supper. What you do with the time I am absent is your own business.'

Abigail perched patiently on the edge of her mother's bed as the maid finished the final steps of her toilette so they might go down to breakfast. Normally she enjoyed the opportunity to sit quietly, unobserved and non-contributing, listening to her mother chattering about the day to come. But after last night, she was full of questions that she did not know how to ask.

Was what had happened with Danforth normal? Should she even have allowed it, when he had given no promise of marriage? Most importantly, should she let it happen again?

But it seemed her mother's mind ran in an entirely different direction. 'I hate to admit that you were right,' she said, touching the curls at the back of her head as the maid removed the last of the papers. 'But it is probably for the best that there is no renewal of Lord Danforth's suit.'

'Really?' Abby said, trying not to sound disappointed by the answer to her unspoken wishes.

'His behaviour with Lady Beverly last night was quite scandalous,' she said with a disapproving frown.

'I refuse to blame poor Lenore for it. She really is the kindest person. Of course, the Duke is a handsome man and powerful as well. Who knows better than us how hard he is to resist when he gets an idea into his head? Your father approved his request to wed you based on his title alone. If you had not had the sense to run from him, you would have married a drunkard as well as a rake.'

'Perhaps things are not so very bad as they appear,' Abby said, trying not to sound too hopeful.

'That is not what you said about him before the wedding,' her mother reminded her. 'Then I thought it unfair of you. But it is clear that you were right all along. Things being how they are between your father and me, I should have known better than to trust a man.'

Though everyone in London knew the details of her father's infidelity, her mother rarely made mention of it, even one as oblique as this. But Abigail had no reason to protect him. 'It is not fair of you to judge the Duke more harshly based on what Father has done.'

This brought an unbelieving look from her mother. 'You are surprisingly charitable to him this morning.'

'Perhaps I am finally learning from your example,' she said, with all the sincerity she could muster. 'Your treatment of Father has always been more generous than he deserves.'

'Because of him, I have all of this,' she said, making a wide gesture to encompass the house they were in. 'It is only because of his family connections that we were allowed here.'

Abby opened her mouth to remind her that they

had not actually been invited, but her mother continued before she could interrupt. 'If you had not been the daughter of a gentleman, you would never have received a proposal from the Duke. That was not all it could have been, of course. But I still have hopes for you, my dear. I have hopes.'

Thinking of her damaged reputation, her mother looked ready to cry again. Abby waved the maid away and placed the final pins in her mother's hair, using it as an excuse to lay a comforting hand on her shoulder. 'Suppose I do not manage to find a husband, Mama,' Abby said, giving her another gentle pat on the shoulder. 'We must, at least, consider the possibility.'

Her mother gave a watery laugh, staring into the mirror and trying to compose herself. 'Do not be ridiculous, my dear. You will find someone. And then, perhaps, I will come and visit you in your house. It will not be as grand as you would have had with the Duke, of course. But there will be some small bit of space for your old mother, I am sure.' There was a faint wistfulness in her tone, as if she had imagined the future so often that she could see it when she closed her eyes.

Had this been her mother's plan all along? Had she wanted to come away with her after the marriage, to escape her own husband? The thought had never occurred to Abby when she had cried off the wedding. She had been far too concerned with avoiding the fate that her mother had chosen for herself. Now her decision might have trapped them both.

But her mother's future should not have to depend on her own. 'Have you thought of what you might do if Father does not come home?' she said, almost afraid to ask.

'He always comes home,' her mother said, confident though not happy. 'This is not the first time he has been away. It is only the most public. In the end, the money will run out, as it always does, and he will come home.'

Abby could still remember the argument after her father's last sojourn to the Continent, the mutterings about tight purse strings and the petulant anger of a man with no option other than to depend on his wife. 'But the money is yours,' Abby said cautiously. 'Grandfather arranged it all, before he died.'

'Yes,' her mother said, in a way that meant *Yes, but...*

Abby ignored her doubts and gave her an encouraging smile. 'Then you do not have to take him back, when he returns.'

'I would not choose to do that,' her mother said, as if it was the strangest idea she'd ever heard. 'He is my husband.'

'You would not choose to, but you could,' Abby repeated. 'The money is secured in trust and you could do whatever you wanted to with it. There is nothing that Papa can do about it.'

'It takes more than money to live in this world,' the older woman said. Now she was dry-eyed and clearheaded. 'I know this better than most.'

'I know you are not brave,' Abby said, pleased that, for a change, there were no signs of impending tears. 'I can be brave enough for both of us.'

'It is not bravery that I am speaking of,' her mother corrected. 'If courage and money were all I needed, I might have left long ago.'

'Then what is it?'

'Women simply do not live alone, my dear,' she said, staring at Abby as if she had lost all sense. 'It is not done.'

'You would not be alone if I stayed with you,' Abby continued. 'We could buy a small house. We would engage just a few servants: a maid and housekeeper. Even if we left Father the town house, we would be able to manage quite well.'

Her mother gave a sad laugh. 'And what would we do to keep ourselves busy? My dear, if you find the current storm tedious, imagine rain without ceasing. That might as well be our future for the number of invitations we will receive.'

A life outside society sounded like heaven. If there were no more invitations, there would be no more embarrassing interactions with strangers, no more gossip that needed to be ignored and no more headaches or stomach aches after an evening of trying to pretend that none of it mattered to her.

It would be fine for her. But she had forgotten her mother's desire to maintain the few advantages her marriage afforded. 'I am sure there are ways to mitigate the stigma. Lady Beverly goes about alone.'

'Lady Beverly is a widow and travels under the protection of the Duke. But if an honest woman who has a husband chooses to live apart from him?' Her mother shook her head. 'It would be easier if I had family instead of money. But if I leave your father, I will have you and you will have me. That is all. All the money in the world will not open doors once they have closed to us.'

'It would be all right,' Abby insisted. 'I do not need so very much.'

'What you need is a husband,' her mother insisted. 'A man who will give you a place in society.'

And you as well. She had been a fool to jilt the Duke. At the time, she had thought only of herself. It appeared that she had been wrong about his tepid feelings for her. But even if things had been as bad as she'd suspected, could it really have been any worse than what her mother faced each day? 'Then I will do my best to find a someone,' she said. And, should there be another offer from the man she'd rejected, she knew what her answer would be.

This made her mother smile. 'It does my heart good to hear you say so. Like it or not, my dear, we are defined by the men that choose us,' she said. 'You will not do better than Danforth, of course. But while you are here, you must do your best not to make an enemy of him.'

'Of course, Mama,' she said, wondering what the lady would think if she knew the truth.

Chapter Eleven

That morning, the rain stopped for almost an hour. The brief respite had the guests in the breakfast room talking optimistically of a walk through the gardens, or at least the luxury of standing by an open window. But by noon, it had begun to pour again and a deep ennui had fallen over the group in the salon. The men did not bother themselves with billiards and the women had had more than enough of cards. Conversation was not worth the effort, either, since so much of it had been expended earlier, speculating about the weather.

Then the distant sound of a slamming door broke the oppressive silence of the room. It was immediately followed by the sound of footsteps hammering down the main stairs and across the hallway towards the dining room. It was a wonder that they could hear the person at all, for the stairs were solid marble and the hallway heavily carpeted to muffle just the sort of noise they had heard.

Abby watched as the women around her looked up

from their needlework like a herd of startled deer, trying to find the exact source of the commotion. The men were only slightly less interested, setting aside their books and newspapers, uncrossing their legs and leaning forward.

'There you are!' an angry male voice bellowed. The announcement was followed by an unintelligible female whimper.

Now the crowd was looking from one to another, counting heads and trying to guess the identity of the culprits. Danforth was missing. If he was not there, it was no surprise that Lady Beverly was gone as well. Abby held her breath, reminding herself that it need not mean anything. But all around her, eyebrows raised and heads nodded.

Then the group considered and gave a collective shrug of denial. Danforth would never raise his voice, nor did the Marchioness ever cry.

'If we are sharing a room, I should not be seeing you for the first time after breakfast.'

The statement was followed by another whimper.

This led to another round of attendance-taking from the guests. Comstock and his wife were not with them, either. But the man shouting in the dining room was not an American, nor had that couple shared a cross word in the whole time they had been there.

Another quick search of the room had the guests mouthing the name *Elmstead* to nods of assent. Lord Elmstead was a ruddy-faced man with a large belly and thick, red hair. His wife was barely twenty-five, slight, blonde and pretty. People frequently commented on the poorly matched pair and pitied the girl for being trapped in marriage to him.

But then, people commented on everything else. It was hardly a surprise.

There was more shouting from the hall. 'If you were indisposed, I would assume your bed was the place for you, not a fainting couch in the dressing room.'

The excuse sounded convincing enough to the ladies in the salon, who were whispering votes of sympathy even as they strained to hear her answers. At a difficult time of month, who among them did not occasionally move to a neighbouring room to avoid disturbing their husband's sleep? And Lady Elmstead was declared vivacious rather than flirtatious. She was not the sort of woman that people accused of infidelity, though many could see why a husband such as hers might tempt her to stray.

Rather than another comment from Elmstead, the next words spoken were from another man, quiet enough to be indistinguishable except for their moderate tone and the American cadence in the accent. Lord Comstock had gone to inform the couple that their argument could be heard and to suggest discretion in the future.

The listeners sighed in disappointment, for it appeared that the day's entertainment was about to end. But then their hostess entered, favoured them all with an excessively bright smile and shut the door behind her, blocking out her husband's attempt to mediate the marital contretemps down the hall. 'You have all been cooped up in this room for too long. I have a delightful way to pass the time. Who fancies a parlour game?' Lady Comstock's voice was far too loud for the crypt-like silence in the room and there was something in her direct gaze that informed them she expected nothing less than full participation.

Her guests offered an unenthusiastic assent.

She gave them another toothy smile to reinforce the fact that participation was mandatory. 'Hide and-seek.' She clapped her hands together as if responding to non-existent approval from her guests. She scanned the room. 'We must have more than one quarry. You, you, and you,' she said, pointing to the two Williams sisters and the young gentleman at their side. 'Off you go. Find hiding places. Separately, please,' she added, wagging her finger. 'The house is large. Feel free to use all of it. There is no need to pile into the same cupboard together and get into mischief. Now, the three of you, get as far away from me... I mean, as far from here as it is possible to go. I shall count to a hundred. Then we shall release the hounds.'

When they did not go immediately, she shooed them towards the door. 'Run along. Anywhere except the nursery, of course. The baby is sleeping. And avoid the library, as well. It is dusty. You will not like it.'

When she had cleared them from the room, she began to count. As the numbers increased, the enthu-siasm for the idea grew. By the time she had reached one hundred, the group had convinced themselves that it was a capital idea and was wondering why they had not thought of it sooner. They headed out, in singles and pairs, laughing and chatting, the fracas in the hall completely forgotten.

The Countess stood in the doorway, waving them off. As Abby passed her, she murmured in a voice so low that it could barely be heard, 'Off you go, the lot of you. If I had known that the company would be as bad as the weather, I'd have locked myself in the library and refused to send the invitations.'

Abby stifled a smile and hurried past her. But before she cleared the doorway, the Countess spoke again, in a clear, commanding voice. 'Miss Prescott. A word, please.'

She turned back. 'Your ladyship?'

The Countess slipped past her and shut the door. Then she turned, leaning with her back to the panels as if she could hold her guests at bay. For a moment, she seemed to have forgotten that Abby was still there. She sighed, then smiled. 'Gone at last. I shall have several hours of peace from this, if we are lucky.'

Abby glanced out the window at the rain that prevented her escape, imagining the inn where she might have been staying without causing anyone bother. 'I must say again that I am sorry to intrude. It appears that you are growing tired of having company and we have only added to your troubles.'

The Countess waved away her apology. 'You and your mother are a welcome diversion for all of us. I had planned activities to keep the party busy. Shooting, riding and croquet. But this blasted weather has trapped us like rats in a cage.' She brightened. 'Or rather, a maze. I should have suggested this days ago.

Someone will invariably get lost in the house. With luck, they will not be missed until supper.'

'I should probably join them,' Abby said, glancing over the Countess's shoulder at the closed door.

'In time,' her hostess replied. 'First, I apologise for my rudeness, just now. I prefer a quiet life, alone in the library with my husband, my daughter and my books. But now that I am the wife of a peer, it is part of my job to be a gracious hostess. If Comstock had not turned out to be so utterly perfect, I would never have taken this on.' She gave Abby a knowing smile. 'Of course, you more than all of us understand the troubles you take on when you fall in love with a peer.'

'I beg your pardon?'

'With Danforth, my dear. You clearly adore him. But you jilted him because you were afraid that he might make you a laughing stock, as your father does your mother.'

'I have no idea what you are talking about,' she lied. The fact that it was true did not make it any less rude of the Countess to point it out.

'People talk, of course. And when they do, you grow wan, your palms sweat on your wine glass, you touch your temple as if you are in pain and you refuse to eat, as if you fear that your meal will not stay in your stomach. You hide it well, of course. But all the same...'

It was an apt list of the symptoms that plagued her when she was out in society. But that did not mean she had to admit to them.

'There are probably guests that are talking about you right now,' the Countess added.

It had not been necessary to speak, for Abby could feel herself paling at the mention. 'Then I had best join them to prevent it,' she replied, glancing towards the door again.

'Or you could find the Duke, as you want to,' the Countess said, with a smile. 'He is no more with Lenore today than he was last night. But you know that, don't you?' She tipped her head to the side and adjusted her spectacles, as if studying Abby. 'There is nothing the least bit romantic about their relationship. You must have learned that by now. But I suspect you have trouble believing it.' She smiled again. 'You have nothing at all to worry about on that front. Lady Beverly will never be more to him than a friend.'

'How can you be sure?' she said, unable to contain her doubts. The Countess was barely acquainted with her and Abby was far too polite to assume a friendship that had not been offered. But Lady Comstock was smiling at her as if they had known each other for years.

The Countess seemed ready to speak. Then she changed her mind and touched a finger to her lips, as if trapping a secret. 'There are some stories that it should not be my job to tell. I suspect you will figure it out on your own, given enough time. But if Danforth has not explained, you should simply ask Lady Beverly.'

'I could never...' There was no etiquette at all that covered questioning another woman about the honesty of the man they shared, especially when the lady had already offered her assurances. Still, there was something in the way the Countess was looking at her that hinted at secrets still not uncovered.

Lady Comstock must have seen the truth in her eyes, for she sighed and stepped away from the door. 'Very well, then. Have it your way and let the mystery remain. But for now, I recommend you use this time to play your own game of hide-and-seek. If you find Danforth, you will have at least some of your answers by supper.'

Then, she stepped out of the way and opened the door. 'If you need me, I will be in the library.' She smiled again. 'But I rather hope you do not need me. My book and my husband are waiting for me and I do not want to disappoint either of them.'

The Countess had made it all sound so easy. All she had to do was ignore things that had bothered her for most of her life and trust blindly in people who had gone out of their way to behave in an untrustworthy manner. Lastly, she had to find the Duke and let him put her mind to rest.

That might be the hardest thing of all. Though the Countess had spoken of his plans as if they were obvious, he had given no indication that he had wanted to see her, today. He had simply disappeared after breakfast, leaving shortly after Lenore, just as he had done on the previous evening. Did he assume that she would go to his room? If so, he was mistaken. Though she wanted to be with him, she was not nearly so desperate as to follow that impulse when there was a game in play that encouraged people to open doors without warning, trying to discover others.

She went to her own bedroom door instead, half-hoping that she would find the Countess's dog, ready to lead her to the place she was supposed to go. But now that she wanted him, the hallway was empty. She stood there for a moment, trying to imagine what he might have meant for her to do.

The thing she feared most was that the answer might be: nothing. Perhaps he was in his room, reading a book. Maybe everything he'd said last night was a lie and he was with Lenore, just as everyone assumed. Or perhaps he was with one of the other guests. Perhaps he had gone on to the next willing female to do much the same thing he had done with her last night. Perhaps what they'd done had been insignificant to him and she was already forgotten.

She balled her fists and pushed them against her temples, trying not to imagine another girl overcome by passion at his touch. He would not do that to her. More importantly, she could not believe that he could carry on another affair without hearing some whisper of gossip about it.

That meant he was either reading in his room as he claimed, or waiting somewhere for her, assuming that she would know how to find him.

Very well, then. She had always thought herself rather good at hide-and-seek. She was simply looking for a different person than everyone else who was playing. At least she need not worry that her behaviour appeared suspicious. As long as the game was in progress, she had the perfect excuse for being in places she should not.

She walked slowly to the back wing, to the room where she had met him last night. The door was still unlocked, but when she opened it, the room was empty. She stood on the threshold for a moment, thinking. She doubted that the Duke of Danforth was the sort of person to hide under the bed. But then she had not expected him to be crawling around in the hall on his hands and knees, either.

Cautiously, she lifted the edge of the coverlet and peeked beneath it. There was nothing but dust. Likewise there was no one in the cupboard or behind the curtains. Logic dictated that she had been wrong. But she had been led this far by something stronger than the rational mind. Even though the room seemed empty, she was sure she was in the right place.

She looked about her again, then walked to the back wall. There was a small ring above the bedside table, too low to be a coat hook or candle holder. She ran her fingers along the papered panels until she found a vertical crack and felt a faint draught tickling her palm.

A secret passage? She smiled. It was not Danforth's house. Yet, in leading her here, it felt as if he had given her some sort of gift. It was as if some part of him understood how much she would enjoy the surprise of it and the chance to explore a space where the rest of the party could not or would not follow.

She hooked her finger into the ring and the panelling pulled away to reveal a lit candle tied to a piece of red cord. When she took the taper down and waved the light around, it revealed a passageway running between the walls. The string appeared to be threaded into a series of staples in the lathe, disappearing into the darkness at the end of the candle's reach.

It was a guide of some sort. Had Danforth left it for her, or had it been there all along? And where might it go, if she followed it?

She smiled again. There was no 'if' involved. She could not resist the temptation. She slipped the candle from the loop at the end and moved forward, letting the cord trail between her fingers as she went. She tried to imagine where it was taking her in relation to the room she had left, but it took only a turn or two before she was totally lost. A chill came over her as she realised that she was completely dependent on the trail that had been left for her. Should she lose track of the cord or drop her candle, she might never see daylight again.

Hope returned as she came to a flight of stairs and a slight lessening of the total darkness in which she had been walking. The narrow corridor widened into a gloomy hallway that led to a pair of dusty glass doors, one of which stood open in what she hoped was welcome.

She walked the last steps slowly. After the darkness of the upper passages, the light shining through the doorway was a welcome relief. But it had a strange, watery quality that was not precisely frightening, but otherworldly, as if she had been enchanted without noticing and wandered into the land of the fey.

Then she felt the change in the air. What had seemed musty before, now smelled of greenery and damp earth. The space around her was no longer silent. She could hear the sound of rain on windows again, but much louder than it had been in the rest of the house, as if the drizzle fell on a hundred panes of glass, instead of just one or two.

She smiled, for she knew what she would see, before she had even stepped over the threshold. The house had a conservatory, a glass house hidden far away from the rooms that the Comstocks had opened to their guests. It was clearly unused, for it lacked the warmth of a proper hothouse. But though there would be no strawberries or oranges from it, the more persistent plants had survived without care. A jungle of withered palms sprouted from the remains of broken pots. Ivy twined in and out of the panes of cracked glass. Now that she was closer to the damaged windows, she could smell the woodbine growing just outside and the fresh scent of the rain.

She stared up for a moment and smiled. The storm had seemed oppressive when she had been in the drawing room with the other guests. But here, the combination of overgrown foliage and sunlight flickering through the water streaming down the transparent roof was wondrous.

'You like it?'

She walked forward, again, pushing aside an oversized fern to find a little clearing in the centre of the room. The leaves on the floor had been covered with a carriage blanket. And there sat a wicker hamper draped with a linen napkin. The Duke stood to one side, working the cork out of a bottle of wine. Two empty glasses waited on a bench next to him.

'A picnic?' she said, amazed.

'I am sure, had the weather been better, we would have gone on one by now,' he said.

'I would not have been here, had there not been a storm,' she reminded him.

He shrugged, and the cork came free with a pop. 'Then, perhaps we would have gone on one had we married.' He glanced at her thoughtfully. 'You are not opposed to them for some reason, are you?'

'I do not think so,' she said. 'I have never been on one.'

'Never?'

'My mother is of a mind that, when one has the money for silver and crystal, one should not have to eat on the ground.' But when confronted with a member of the peerage so at ease, the prohibition seemed unnecessarily prim.

He poured the wine and offered her a glass before sitting down on the blanket and stretching his legs out before him. 'I have no intention of forgoing Comstock's crystal, but the silver will not be needed. Eating without it is half the novelty of picnicking.' He pulled a whole cold pheasant from under the cloth and began to dismember it with his fingers.

'What else do you have?' she asked, kneeling on the rug to peer into the basket.

'Bread, cheese, teacakes. And grapes.'

She helped herself to a cake and made herself comfortable on the floor beside him. 'How ever did you manage this?'

'I simply went down to the kitchen and asked for it.' He grinned. 'They were sufficiently uncomfortable to have a duke hanging about the fire that they would have given me anything I asked for, just to get me to leave. They may be forced to put up with Comstock's American egalitarianism, but I doubt such tolerance extends to me.'

She smiled and shook her head. 'I mean, how did you manage to get it all to the room? The passage was quite narrow. There was barely enough space for me. Come to that, how did you find the passage at all? It was quite well hidden.'

'Comstock showed it to me,' he said with a grin. 'There are limits to the number of billiard games one can play before going completely mad. And as for this?' He gestured to the food arranged on the blanket. 'I made two trips. It was necessary to balance the basket on my head for part of the way. You'd have been in awe of my abilities, had you seen it.'

It was obviously true for his normally perfect hair was mussed and there was a smudge of dust on the knee of his breeches. He could just as easily have commanded a team of footmen arrange it all for him. Instead, he had done it all himself, just to impress her.

And it had worked. She felt a strange fluttering in her heart, quite different from the desire she was accustomed to feeling when she looked at him. It grew even stronger when she remembered the way he'd treated the maid and her broken necklace. She had thought him overly proud before they were to be married and distant in social situations. But when she'd seen him alone, he was not the least bit pretentious. It was not so very surprising that he might go to the kitchen himself, should he wish for something special to be prepared. 'Do you behave this way when you are at home?'

'In what way?' he said, puzzled.

'Doing for yourself. What do your servants think about your behaviour?'

He laughed. 'I suspect Gibbs would give notice immediately, should I try to tie my own cravat. I could not possibly perform to his standards. But I am not above conversing with the footmen and maids, and can find my way to the kitchen, should I wish a snack. Most of the staff have known me since I was a child,' he said. 'Since I was but sixteen when I inherited the title, many of them cannot quite believe that I am now a full-grown man.'

'So young,' she whispered. 'How did you manage?'

'I had no other choice but to do so,' he said. 'Though I continued to sneak biscuits from the kitchen, I made a point of being circumspect in other aspects of my life. I learned to listen more than I spoke. My silence allowed people to assume a depth of character that I did not, at first, have.'

'You must have seemed a very serious young man,' she said. It explained why he had grown into such a reserved adult.

But today he smiled. 'I suspect everyone preferred my behaviour to that of my father. He was an absolute tartar to both family and servants.' He said it in an offhand manner, as if living with such a man was no trouble at all.

She stared at him in amazement, for she knew otherwise.

'Have I done something to surprise you?' he said.

'Since arriving at this house, you have done nothing but surprise me,' she said. Not only was more he open and talkative than he had been, with this secluded luncheon he had set a scene which seemed quite proper on one hand and ripe for seduction on the other.

His smile now looked smug. 'Good. It will not do to be too predictable in courting you, I think. Would you like a grape?'

She held up a hand. 'We are courting, then?'

'I thought you knew.' He held the fruit out to her, rolling it between his fingers in a way that made her nipples tighten.

'To what end?' she said, forcing herself to look into his eyes and not at his clever hands.

'I still hope to make you my Duchess,' he said, popping the grape into his own mouth.

Now she was watching his lips, imagining his tongue on her body. 'Does that mean you have forgiven me for the way our last engagement ended?'

'I blame myself for that,' he said, reaching into the basket for another grape. 'I assumed that my title was enough to guarantee success of the union.'

'With most women, it would have been,' she allowed. It should have been. She had been informed of that often enough. But she had wanted him to speak freely, a thing he had trained himself never to do. 'I am sorry that I disappointed you.'

He touched her hand. 'Do not be. Since seeing you again, I have decided that such a shallow acceptance was not enough for me,' he replied, giving her a significant look. He was not precisely staring, but the level of interest when he looked at her had changed in the few days that they had been talking. In London, she had been convinced that she bored him. But now he was definitely interested in her and not just because he wished to do the things he'd suggested last night.

'Why did you propose to me the last time?'

'So many questions,' he said, holding out the grape to her.

She reached for it and he pulled his hand away, then offered it again, his hand extending to touch her lips.

She closed her eyes and took it, trying to ignore the faint warmth of his hand and concentrate on the pop of the skin and the burst of sweetness on her tongue. She swallowed and looked at him again. 'You have not answered me.'

He shrugged. 'It is a bad habit of mine.'

'I am aware of that,' she said, helping herself to another grape. 'But you promised to do better than you did the first time you proposed, so you must indulge at least some of my curiosity.'

He responded with a nod of acquiescence.

'When you offered for me, we were strangers. I had no idea what I had done to attract your attention, nor do I understand this renewal.'

This seemed to surprise him. But rather than annoyance, the puzzlement turned into the slightest of smiles. 'I am not used to having my motives questioned.'

'Then I doubt we will do well together,' she said, pushing her plate aside. 'For I will do so frequently. You cannot expect me to walk blindly through the rest of my life, trusting that you know what is best for both of us, especially since you've made no effort to discover my likes or dislikes, needs or wants.'

'Until now,' he reminded her. 'Lenore says that, because of my title, I am too used to having my own way.'

'And apparently I have to tell you that it is never good to mention one lady while courting another,' Abby replied. 'Especially when it is your goal to convince her that she has no rival.'

'Very true,' he said, nodding again. 'My apologies, Miss Prescott.' Then he smiled in a way that showed his confidence had returned. 'Or, after what has happened between us already, might I call you Abigail?'

She could not help the blush creeping into her cheeks as she said, 'I prefer Abby. Abigail makes me sound like a maid.'

He nodded. 'Very well, Abby, you wished to know why I offered for you.'

'And why you continue to pursue me,' she added. 'And do not tell me that it is because I am pretty. There are girls making their come out this Season who are far prettier and who have more advantageous connections, as well. But you did not wish to marry any of them.'

'Possibly true,' he agreed. 'But beauty is a matter

of personal taste and I cannot think of any female in a decade of Seasons that I consider finer than you.'

'Oh.' Was it possible to be both flattered and disappointed at the same time? If this was the answer to her question, it was far less than she had hoped to hear.

Then he smiled again. 'That said, it was not the main thing that attracted me to you. Do you remember the night we met?'

'If you are speaking of the ball at Almack's, we did not actually meet,' she pointed out.

'But you do you remember it, just as I do,' he said. There was warmth in his voice, as he recalled it, as if it was possible to savour a moment, like a glass of good brandy.

'We did not speak, nor were we introduced.' That was what she'd told herself on the carriage ride home. And later that night, when she could not stop thinking of him.

'And yet I liked to think we had met,' he said, his conviction unshaken. 'I watched you, discreetly, for the rest of the evening. I was waiting for you to do something that would bring me to my senses. Instead, I saw the way you dealt with your father's temper.'

That night, she had been so busy wondering about him that she'd almost managed to forget the rest of the evening. 'He was angry that we were late,' she said.

'You were not the success he'd hoped,' the Duke added.

The reminder of it stung. That night, she'd told herself that most of the available gentlemen were busy with other ladies. But there had been a niggling fear that there was something about her that had repelled their interest. 'Was your offer made to console me?' she said, confused.

He shook his head and his smile became a grin of admiration. 'You did not seem to need my help. When your father badgered you over it, you said you would throw a fit on the dance floor to shame him. I believe demonic possession was referenced.'

'Oh.' In retrospect, she was not sure which was more embarrassing, the fact that her words had been overheard, or how near they were to the truth. When she had uttered them, the pressure had been building behind her temples and she had been sure that if her father spoke one more word she would cast up her dinner on the dance floor, or, at the very least, fall into a swoon.

Apparently, it had never occurred to the Duke that she had been in distress for he laughed at the memory. 'I had been preparing to rush to your aid and salvage your night by requesting an introduction. Instead, you put Prescott in his place and he gave you no further trouble.'

'Not until we got home, at least,' she replied. Because her father had learned exactly how much abuse his family could take when they were in public, he was at his worst when there were no witnesses. He had badgered her mother to the edge of tears. Then he had stopped and turned his temper to Abby. 'Father ranted about that evening for almost a week.' And she had stayed in her room with a basin near her head and the curtains drawn against the light. 'But then you arrived with your offer and, suddenly, I could do no wrong.'

Then she had spoiled the wedding and his mood as well. 'I was forced to rusticate after the wedding,' she said, afraid to look up from her wine glass. 'Mama went with me, of course. But Father loathes the country. He had found consolation in the arms of a new mistress.'

'When my father was alive, he was much the same.' His voice was gentle, like the hand of a surgeon, probing a fresh wound. 'Early in life, I realised that it was not possible to get the upper hand against a man who need answer only to the King, so I stopped trying to fight him. I never shouted back at him. I did not contradict him, no matter how wrong he was. I did not frown or laugh or smile or cry. I did not cower in the face of his rage. I simply waited until it stopped.'

'Did he surrender when you refused to argue?' she said, intrigued.

'On the contrary, it made him even angrier. I won in the end, of course. He shouted himself into an apoplexy and died before I reached my majority. Then I took his place as head of the family.'

'It appears that you never lost the habit of hiding your thoughts and feelings,' she said. 'In London, I assumed your aloof nature was because you had no real interest in me.'

'I am not without feelings,' he assured her. 'I simply do not believe in showing them to excess, as my father did. It is quite possible that he'd have lived longer had he not spent all his energy in trying to break me.' He was smiling now, in the same distant way he had as he'd proposed to her, as though his mind was somewhere far away and not nearly so happy.

'It was not your fault he died young,' she said.

He came back to her, then, with the doubtful raise of an eyebrow. 'It was me he was shouting at when he had his final attack. It would not have been so bad if he had gone quickly. But he lingered in a sickbed for some months after he was stricken. He still tried to shout, but his mouth and tongue could no longer work to speak clearly.' There was a brief flash of pain in his eyes, immediately stifled by his iron will. 'He did not really need words. I could understand him well enough. I knew exactly what he wished to say to me.'

'Have you told anyone of this?' she asked in a quiet voice.

'Not even Lenore,' he said, looking faintly surprised again.

It would be easier for both of them if he would cry. After a lifetime with her mother, she knew how to handle tears. Anger as well, thanks to her father. But there was nothing in her life to teach her how to mend pain that she could not even see.

So, she reached out to him in the only way she could think of, putting her arms around his neck and her mouth to his.

His breath was unsteady at first, as though he could not decide whether to take advantage of what she was offering or push her away. It would have been easier for him to tempt her to submission one grape at a time, plying her with wine and cake until her legs spread and her last reservations disappeared.

It would have been wonderful, she was sure, just as the last two kisses had been. But though she had been ready to give all to him, he had kept a part of himself separate from her. Today, she wanted more from him.

He fought that battle for only a few seconds before surrendering to what she wanted. With each passing moment she held him, he seemed to calm, the muscles of his arms and neck growing soft under her hands, before tensing again. Then he gathered her to him and stretched out on the blanket, pulling her down to lay beside him, touching from head to foot. There was a rattle of plates and the tinkling of a spilled glass as his free arm swept the picnic out of the way. Then there was nothing but the crunch of dry leaves under their bodies and the twinned sounds of their breathing.

After a time, the kiss ended and he touched her face, brushing the hair from her eyes and tracing the curve of her parted lips with his thumb. She responded in kind, grazing his cheek with her knuckles and feeling the beginnings of stubble. Then, as she had with the kiss, she led the way, stroking his shoulders and slipping her hands under his coat, unbuttoning his waistcoat to rest her palms on the linen of his shirt, dragging her fingertips down his body until they caught under the top band of his breeches.

He let out another shaky sigh and reached to undo his buttons, letting the flap of his pants fall. She knew his manhood must be there, just within reach, but she could not bring herself to look away from his face. His eyes were closed, his mouth unsmiling, lips parted, moving as if in silent prayer. He was waiting for her to decide what she wanted from him.

It was unfair of him to leave this to her, when he knew that she did not know what was supposed to happen next. But if she admitted defeat, the part of him that she most wanted would retreat, to be replaced by the man he showed to others: cool, efficient and invulnerable. So, she did as she had done before and led blindly.

She took her hands away from his waist. With one she raised her skirts and with the other she dragged his hand beneath them, placing it on the bare skin of her thigh. Then she reached out with both hands and cradled his manhood in them.

His eyelids flew open and his shocked gaze locked with hers, eyes widening as she began to explore, feeling the soft skin grow hard and tight over blood and muscle. His whole body jerked in surprise as she stroked him from root to tip and his other hand plunged forward, beneath her petticoats, then froze as it closed on the crease at the top of her leg.

She stroked again, harder this time, running a nail along the skin at the head of him, silently daring him to go further.

In response, he sucked a breath through his teeth as if struggling to maintain control. Then his hand relaxed and his knuckles grazed the folds between her legs. He parted them with his thumb and with a single touch, she could feel herself move closer to release. His hand moved again and his fingers slid into her, claiming her body as his own.

It was very, very good, but it was not the sudden rush of pleasure that she'd felt when he had kissed her in the bedroom upstairs. He was toying with her, prolonging the play, waiting for…something. Then she understood. She had the power to make him do whatever she pleased.

She tightened her grip on him, pretending that her hands were her body, making a channel of them, enveloping him. His legs were shaking, his hips bucking under her ministrations. But his fingers began to move inside her, trying to gain control of her before he lost his.

He would fail. Because this time, she refused to let him win until he had given her every part of himself. He was near to breaking, his expression desperate, his breath coming in gasps, then released slowly as he tried not to give in to her.

She closed her eyes, pretending to surrender, and wet her lips, biting the lower one with her teeth as she concentrated on how he felt in her hands and imagining how it might feel to have him where his fingers were, buried to the part that was now cupped and resting heavy in one of her hands. He would move in her like the slide of her hand on him now and her muscles would hold him inside, just…like…this.

Suddenly, his whole body stiffened, then went limp as he gave a final groan and spent himself in her hand. She opened her eyes then, to find his face not defeated, but triumphant. His smile was almost a grimace of pain, his cheeks wet with sweat or tears as if, by touching him, she had wrung every last feeling out of him along with his release.

There was a moment of utter stillness between them. Then, his hands began to work against her. They were gentle now, relaxed and sure. But they were no less possessive. One of his thumbs went unerringly to the most sensitive place, circling it as his fingers slipped deep inside her again.

'Good?' he asked. He sounded as breathless as she felt. Was that what she had done to him? She nodded. It was very good. It was even better than the last time. When she was sure that he had done all he could to her, still he did not stop, moving faster, making her beg. Making her break as he had done.

He did not withdraw as she came back to herself. But then she had not released him, either. He was still resting safely against her palm as they stared into each other's eyes.

'This was not what I had planned for the afternoon,' he said, his composure returning, though the smile accompanying it was not quite so unreadable.

'What were you intending?' she said.

'Just a picnic,' he said, trying to look innocent. 'And to let nature take its course.'

She must have looked confused for he laughed. 'I thought, perhaps, I might try to seduce you.'

'With grapes?' she said, remembering how he had been feeding her before.

'I knew it was unwise. You are an innocent young lady, after all.'

'Am I, still?' she said, suddenly doubtful.

'You have stumbled upon a game that is much more fun than hide-and-seek,' he said, moving his fingers inside her body. 'And far safer than the one I might have attempted.'

It was hard to imagine that real lovemaking might be more risky than this, for what was happening did not feel safe at all. What they had done was wet and messy and dangerous. It was broad daylight. They were both half-naked. And she suspected that, in the throes of passion, she might have sat on a teacake.

But she could feel her body waking again, with each movement he made, and the organ in her hand seemed to be waking as well. And the Duke of Danforth was looking at her with a hopeful smile that made her want to call him Benedict and agree to anything he might suggest.

'How long?' she said, half-whispering.

'How long for what?' he responded.

'How long until we are missed?' she asked, not sure whether she was more hopeful or worried.

He consulted his pocket watch. 'An hour at least.' The smile he gave her next almost stopped her heart. 'And that, my darling Abigail, is all the time in the world.'

Chapter Twelve

Benedict had never noticed how beautiful the rain was.

He had first become aware of it while staring up at the roof of the Comstock conservatory after Abigail Prescott had proved to him how little he knew about women and about love. How had an inexperienced girl managed to shatter his control so completely, breaking through barriers that it had taken years to build with a touch of her hand?

It explained much about the barely understood fears he'd had when he had offered for her in London. He had thought to get her properly married and spirited away to the Danforth country property before the process of seduction had even begun. He would be teacher, she would be student. The doors to his heart could be opened slowly as he grew accustomed to the companionship of the woman who would share the rest of his life.

He had not imagined an apt pupil that would surpass his teaching before they'd even reached the final lesson, stripping him naked to the soul with a kiss.

She had ruined him. Reduced him to one of those lovestruck fools who stared at darkening windowpanes and imagined the raindrops on them were diamonds, then wished he could collect them to lay at his lady's feet. When Lenore saw him, she would laugh out loud.

And he would laugh with her, for he did not care what she thought.

'You look to be in an exceptionally good mood, Your Grace.' He could tell that it was Lady Sanderson speaking without even turning around. He could hear the sound of her restrung pearls slicking together as she toyed with them.

'I had a very satisfying afternoon nap,' he said, trying not to look as smugly happy as he felt.

'I was given to understand that you had gone to your room to read a book,' she said. Her tone was probing and bordered on impolite interest.

He turned away from the window to address her directly. 'I did. And when I finished it, I fell asleep.' He made a point to avoid lying, even about such small things as this. He had, indeed, read the final chapter before going down to the conservatory. And there had been a brief but delicious nap, as well, taken in the arms of the beautiful woman who had loved him to completion.

'Well, it has done you good. You are positively brimming with vitality,' she said with a knowing grin.

'Thank you,' he replied, making a mental note to police his moods even more closely than he had before. It was one thing to be in love and quite another to look like it. If he wished to keep Abby free of the gossip she detested, he would have to school himself not to sigh over raindrops until their second engagement had been announced in *The Times*.

'Lady Beverly had a nap as well,' Lady Sanderson added.

'How fortunate for her,' he replied.

'But it must have been very short. When the games started, she was seen hurrying down the bedroom hall, away from her own room,' Lady Sanderson said, staring at him as if she expected a response.

Though he had his suspicions, he had no idea exactly who Lenore had been visiting when she was not with him, nor did he particularly care. Even if he had, he would not want to share the information with this busybody. He schooled his face into his most impassive expression and stared at her, waiting.

'Lady Beverly's room is next to yours, is it not?'

'It usually is,' he said. There was no point in denying the fact, for they always requested rooms that were adjoining and sometimes received a connecting suite. It was assumed that they would make use of the convenience. Until now, the other guests had been polite enough to pretend that they had not noticed.

'How interesting,' she said. 'I hope Lady Beverly was not lost. It is a very big house, you know. So many doors…'

'Indeed,' he said, staring back at her without emotion.

'Perhaps I should ask her.'

'Do as you please,' Benedict answered, continuing to stare at the woman until she and her damned pearls moved away. Then, he followed her movements around the room, watching her interrogate each guest in turn, paying an annoying amount of attention to several young ladies. If she got to Abby, it was doubtful that their afternoon activities would remain secret for long under such rigorous questioning.

But before that interview could occur, Lenore had gone to Abigail's side, asking a few brief questions and pointing her towards the door. Then she wandered in Benedict's direction, laid a languid arm upon his shoulder and whispered in his ear, 'It appears that Lady Sanderson is not satisfied with the usual gossip in this house. She has decided to fish for more.'

'Your fault, this time. You were seen outside someone's room and it was not mine.'

Lenore responded with an indifferent shrug. 'Do not blame me for this. You look as though you were struck directly in the nether regions by Cupid's sharpest arrow and Miss Prescott cannot stop staring at you.'

'What did you say to her?'

'I sent her off to the library to retrieve a book that I have assured her is a personal favourite. The Comstocks have a most unusual collection, full of things no young lady should be seen with.'

'Then why in God's name did you direct her towards it?' he snapped, before gaining control of his temper again.

'Because it will give her a reason for her blush,' she said, staring towards the door as she waited for Abby's return. 'It will also re-establish my claim upon you, Danforth.'

'You have no claim upon me,' he said, brushing her hand off his shoulder.

'But for the sake of a certain innocent party, I do not want people knowing that fact until we are safely away from here,' she said in an urgently sincere tone unlike her usual devilish good humour.

'Might I remind you that Abby Prescott is innocent as well?'

Lenore arched an eyebrow. 'Is she really, Danforth? Because she looks well tumbled to me.'

'No matter how old it is, our friendship does not entitle you to speak that way about my future wife.'

'The engagement is back on?' she said, surprised, but clearly happy for him.

Then he remembered how little talking had been done that afternoon. 'Not officially,' he allowed.

'Then if you can manage to keep your hands off her and woo her like a proper gentleman, you and I should be able to maintain our charade for a few more days,' Lenore said with a small sigh. 'And here she is now.'

Abby had entered, carrying a small leather volume, only to be stopped immediately by Lady Sanderson.

Benedict stared at the book in her hand, then back at Lenore. 'What did you send her after?'

'*Thérèse Philosophe*,' she said, covering her mouth with her hand to hide the smile.

'Dear God.' Benedict said, starting forward to grab the book out of her hand.

Lenore held him gently by the arm. 'Do not trouble yourself that she will be corrupted by a book before you get your chance with her. I made sure before I sent her that she does not speak French.' Lenore gave her a speculative glance. 'Unless you wish me to teach her...'

'You have done too much already,' he said, glaring at her. 'And my concern is not that she will read it. Suppose Lady Sanderson reads French?'

There was a sudden shriek and the clatter of loose pearls hitting the floor.

'She does,' Lenore said, triumphantly. 'And now she has quite forgotten whatever it was she was sniffing after.' Then, she laughed out loud, elbowing him in the ribs as if urging him to laugh along with a joke that he wanted no part in.

Abby turned to them now, her face not just blushing, but crimson with embarrassment. She looked from him to Lenore and back again, her eyes narrowing in suspicion and her flush turning to anger.

He shook his head in denial before remembering his plan to keep what they had done a secret. He could not let her go on thinking that he had any part in what had just happened.

But no one noticed him, for, as his friend had predicted, any previous scandal was completely dismissed. 'Oh, dear,' Lenore said, not sounding the least bit guilty. 'Whatever have I done? I believe Lady Sanderson has fainted. Hartshorn?' she called. 'Does anyone have any hartshorn?'

Apparently, the lady now on the floor was not the only French speaker. There was another shriek, more than one giggle, and a wail of misery from Abby's mother.

Beneath it all, the Countess muttered to her husband, 'And this was why I suggested we get a lock for the library door.'

Abby was the only one silent in the room. Her cheeks had gone from red to chalky white and her hand was against her mouth. Looking almost as if she meant to be sick, she pushed her way through the guests crowding around Lady Sanderson and ran for the door.

Before she reached it, Benedict caught her arm. 'Miss Prescott.'

'Let me go,' she whispered and pulled her arm free.

'I had nothing to do with what just happened,' he said.

'But your friend did,' she said, practically spitting the words at him.

'She was trying to spare you attention over...'

'She was trying to embarrass me,' Abby corrected. 'And she succeeded.'

'Lady Sanderson was about to discover what we had done.'

'If she had, you might have been forced to offer for me,' she said. 'Why would that be a problem? Unless it had been your intention all along to forget me as soon as we leave here.'

'Of course, I mean to marry you,' he said. 'But I thought you would not want to be forced into accepting me because of a scandal.'

'Nor do I wish to be made a laughing stock by the woman everyone but you believes to be your lover.'

'Not everyone,' he insisted. 'You know the truth.'

'Does Lenore?' she asked with a sardonic smile.

'Of course. There is nothing between us and there never will be. We have an agreement.'

'And now that you are about to break it, she is trying to destroy me,' Abby said.

'She is trying to protect...' Someone. Even he was not sure who.

'She is lying to you, Benedict. You are a fool to believe otherwise. And I am an even bigger fool to trust either of you.' He reached for her again and she dodged his hand, running for the stairs. But before he could follow, the door to the salon opened and the guests flooded into the hall, ready for dinner, making further conversation impossible.

Chapter Thirteen

After running from the salon, Abby refused to come down to dinner, telling her mother that she was too ill. It was at least partly true for her stomach roiled at the thought of having to share a table with Lenore, staring at her smug smile of success while Benedict sat only a few feet away, wilfully oblivious.

She had not thought it possible that the nearly perfect afternoon would end with her feeling even worse than she had during the week of their attempted marriage. At least then, she had not thought Benedict cared about her. Now she was sure he did, but that it would not be enough. No matter what their future might be, Lenore would always be standing between them, unwilling to accept that she had lost.

There was a knock at the bedroom door, but she had made her apologies several times already, to both her mother and Lady Comstock, so she ignored it. Then it came again. And a third time when she did not answer that.

'I am indisposed,' she called at last, throwing herself on the bed and pulling a pillow over her ears so she would not have to hear it.

'Then I will not be long.'

Abby let out a scream of frustration, sat up and tossed the pillow she'd been holding at Lady Beverly, who was standing at the foot of her bed. 'I did not give you leave to enter.'

'And I did not ask permission,' she replied. 'But there are things that must be settled between us and I do not have the patience to wait for you to come out of hiding.'

Since it was pointless to deny what she was doing, she responded, 'I would not be in hiding if you had not humiliated me in front of the whole house.'

'And that is why I came to apologise,' her adversary replied, her hands in an open gesture of surrender.

It was the last thing that Abby had expected to hear and she could not think of a way to answer it.

Lenore continued. 'I am sorry. Truly. I am accustomed to playing such games with Danforth and forget how they must seem to others.'

'Games?' Abby said, baffled.

'Since he tends to be stoic in the face of anything that may occur, he is the perfect foil for those moments when I choose to do something outrageous as a distraction.' Then she looked at Abby. 'But you have changed him.'

'I did nothing,' she insisted, trying to forget how he had looked when they had parted after their picnic.

'Did you not see how he was behaving tonight? Just as he was after he proposed to you in London. He does not know up from down,' Lenore said with a laugh. 'And you? What the two of you were doing this afternoon was writ plain on your face as you entered the salon before dinner. If you mean to spend your afternoons in dalliance, you will have to learn to hide it better.'

It was pointless to deny something that Lenore had helped arrange, so she said, 'Did you embarrass me as a punishment for what we had done?'

Lenore laughed again. 'Good heavens, no. You might assume I am behaving as I do out of jealousy, but I was quite happy to be elsewhere during your little tête-à-tête. Unfortunately, I was seen in a place I had no business being by the same woman who was about to question you.'

'You were having a liaison?' Abby said, surprised.

Lenore nodded. 'With someone I like very well, who I do not wish to hurt by my carelessness. And that old biddy with the pearls had decided to hound us all until she discovered the truth,' Lenore replied. 'I am sorry to have involved you in the solution without explanation. But I suspect, after this afternoon, she will have forgotten entirely the questions she meant to ask you about Danforth's intentions.'

'You were trying to help me?' Abby said, still suspicious.

Lenore nodded. 'From this point forward, if you behave strangely, or blush without explanation—' she shrugged '—our friends will put it all down to the prurient nature of your reading material.'

'What was in that book?' she asked, afraid of what the answer would be.

Lenore gave an airy wave of her hand. 'A convent

girl is debauched by her priest, among others.' She smiled. 'Since telling you even that much has made you blush, I chose well.'

If she did not have a megrim when she'd come to the room, Abby suspected that one would develop should she spend any more time with Lady Beverly. 'Very well. You have explained your behaviour.' She glanced past her towards the door, willing her to say goodbye.

'We are not quite done speaking yet,' Lenore replied.

'Since I have nothing more to say to you, I cannot think of any reason for you to remain,' Abby said, standing and walking to the door to see her out.

'You are young and in love, and Danforth being what he is, he has not told you all you need to know about our relationship, probably claiming it is a matter of honour.'

'Yes,' Abby said, wetting her lips again and trying to find the right words to ask indelicate questions.

'I would not mind if he told the truth,' she said, with a feline smile. 'But even after all this time, he sometimes has trouble discussing it. In truth, he is rather prudish over such matters.'

'Prudish.' After what they had done this afternoon, it was the last word she would use to describe him.

'I assume he has told you that I am not his mistress,' she said, in a leading tone.

'Yes,' Abby replied, using the same tone back to her.

'But it is clear after today that, no matter how he insists, you will never fully believe him. You are convinced that, even if nothing has happened as yet, it is bound to happen eventually if we continue to spend time in each other's company after your marriage.'

It was an accurate assessment of her fears. 'People will talk,' she replied.

Lenore shook her head. 'There has been nothing. There never will be. It is not that he never loved me. But he understands why we will never be together and made peace with it, ages ago.'

'With your infertility?' Abby said.

Lenore laughed so hard at this that it took some time before she was able to speak. Then she said, 'To the best of my knowledge, the problem in my last marriage was with my husband, who was no more interested in me than I was in him. He had friends at his club and I much prefer the company of women.'

'Most times, they are easier to understand,' Abby said, wishing she would come to the point. 'But that has little to do with the conversation we are having.'

Lenore was staring at her in disbelief. 'Perhaps I should have sent you after a book of poetry by Sappho.'

When she saw that held no meaning either, she spoke in a slow, didactic way, 'When it comes to intimacy, I prefer my own sex.'

Abby frowned, still confused. It almost sounded like she was referring to a romantic relationship. But that could not be right, because Abby was not even sure that such a thing was possible. She puzzled over it for a moment, trying to imagine how it would work.

Then, with a puff of exasperation, Lenore leaned forward, cupped her chin with a long-fingered hand

and kissed her on the mouth in the same way Benedict had, before retreating to leave Abby dazed with shock.

Then, as she so frequently did, Lenore laughed. 'Do you understand now? I have kissed Benedict, long ago, when we were young and foolish. But for me, it was nowhere so pleasant as that. But we have been friends since childhood. When I made him understand that there could never be any more than that between us, he agreed that it might be easier for both of us to keep company and channel any gossip about me far away from the most interesting parts of my life.'

'So, you...' She still could not quite manage to form the words to describe what was happening.

'There are other like-minded ladies in the *ton,* most of whom are married. It is not difficult to meet them at house parties like this while the gentlemen are busy at hunting or fishing or drinking port. It is somewhat harder in bad weather, when we are all trapped inside and getting under each other's feet.'

'And Benedict provides you with an alibi,' she finished.

'It is much easier to get away from the crowd when everyone assumes I am waiting in his bed,' she agreed, smiling.

'And how does he benefit from this arrangement?' Abby asked.

'I do the same for him. Today, when he wished to be with you...'

'Does he have many lovers?'

The question should not have been shocking, but it seemed to surprise Lenore. 'Not many,' she said, at last.

'Fewer than you?' Abby pressed.

Lenore nodded.

'And I suspect he can manage them without your help.'

'In the future, he will have only you,' Lenore said, smiling.

'For the moment, let us speak of the past,' Abby said. 'If he is not always sneaking from room to room, how has this arrangement benefited him?'

For a moment, Lenore looked as confused as Abby had been. 'The poor boy does not like crowds. He would rather sit in his room and read than choke down port with strangers. He does not enjoy sharing himself with people whom he does not know well. It is much easier for him to have a single, close friend to converse openly with then to become intellectually intimate with others,' she said with a flutter of her hands.

'He is not a poor boy,' Abby said softly. 'He is a grown man, very near to your age. He has the power of speech, when he chooses to use it.'

'But it is against his nature to laugh and chat with people who do not have his full trust,' the older woman reminded her. 'His father…'

'Is dead,' Abby finished. 'And has been for quite some time.'

'Sixteen years,' Lenore said, hesitating.

'And who are his other friends?' she asked. 'Are they aware of the reason for your ruse?'

'Other friends,' Lenore said. Then, after a long pause, she added, 'He has acquaintances at his club…'

'Like your husband did?'

'No,' she said hurriedly. 'Not at all like that. He does not speak of them, of course. But I am sure there must be some gentlemen he counts as friends.'

'But you are not sure,' Abby said, beginning to understand why it was so difficult for Benedict to explain this friendship.

'He has always found it easier to remain apart from society,' Lenore confessed.

'Because, as a boy, he feared that they would think him foolish,' Abby said.

'But he is not. He never was. He would rather read than talk. Even when in company, he has little to say,' Lenore insisted.

'Has your friendship made it easier or more difficult to do so?'

Lenore did not have to answer the question for she must know it herself. She was the one who smiled, who chatted and smoothed the edges of any problem while Benedict stood in the corner and observed.

At last, she smiled and shook her head. 'You are smarter than your years, Miss Prescott. I told him that you would be good for him. I am happy to see I was right.'

'Then there will be no more tricks?' she said.

'No more surprises,' Lenore replied. 'Goodnight, Miss Prescott.' And then she was gone, before Abby could realise that her question had not been answered at all.

Chapter Fourteen

The next morning, Benedict lingered in the breakfast room, hoping to see Abby. Though he told himself that she could not hide in her room for ever, he was not totally sure of that fact. The rain had stopped again and the sky had cleared for most of the morning before beginning to cloud over again.

After yesterday, he was sure the Prescotts would be gone the minute the grass was dry. If things remained unsettled between them when she left, he might never convince Abby that his intentions were sincere.

'No sign of her?'

'No thanks to you,' he said. For the first time in his life, Lenore's constant presence annoyed him.

'I apologised,' she said. 'Last night, after dinner, I went to her room and explained.'

'Everything?' he said.

'Everything,' she said, smiling as if this might settle it all. 'She is aware of the details of our arrangement. And she put me in my place. Apparently, she feels that I have been taking advantage of your good nature.'

If she had, it had never bothered him before. But now that he had found Abby, things were different. 'When I marry, some things will have to change between us.'

She nodded, sadly.

'We will still be friends, of course,' he assured her.

'That will never change,' she agreed.

'But in the future, when we are at parties like this, we must be much more careful about our interactions,' he said. 'There must be no more rumours about us.'

Now she was looking at him as if he was a naive child. 'And how do you propose to stop them?'

It was an excellent question.

'If we are discreet, they will die in time, I am sure,' he said.

'Eventually,' she agreed. 'When you have been married as long as we have been together, our supposed affair will be all but forgotten.'

With Abby's dislike of gossip, sixteen years was not soon enough. 'I will think of something,' he said.

'For now, if you are interested, Miss Prescott is in the morning room, reading a book of psalms and trying to repent for her interest in pornography.'

He set his coffee aside and left without bothering to say goodbye.

In the morning room, Abby was sitting by the window, with the psalter open in her lap. In the rare rays of morning sunlight, her dark hair shone like obsidian and the blush that still lingered on her pale cheeks made her look like a repentant fallen angel.

He wanted to make the room believe that nothing improper had happened between them. But ignoring her was likely to be more suspicious and not less. So, he approached her, as any gentleman might, gestured to the chair at her side and said, 'Miss Prescott, is this seat taken?'

She looked up, colouring attractively and answered in a near whisper, 'No, Your Grace.'

'I do not mean to interrupt,' he said, not caring whether others in the room might hear. 'But I understand that my friend Lenore played a cruel trick on you yesterday.'

'She has already apologised to me,' Abby replied, giving him a desperate look of warning.

'All the same, I feel I owe you an apology as well.' He could feel ears all over the room pricking to catch their conversation, even though it could not be more mundane. 'No matter what has happened between us in the past, I would not want you to be hurt because of your acquaintance with me.'

'That is most kind of you, Your Grace.' The words were right, but they sounded too formal and there was none of the warmth in her voice that he had heard in the conservatory. Was she trying to conceal her feelings because they were being observed? Or had she only accepted his apology to avoid talk?

'Not kind at all,' he said, choosing his words carefully. 'It is no less than you deserve. In fact, I would like…'

Before he could finish his attempt at a discreet reconciliation, there was another commotion in the hall.

'I should not have to hunt through the whole of this house each time I wish to ask you a question!'

Elmstead was shouting at his wife again and the guests gathered in the morning room were torn between curiosity and frustration at the repetitive argument. Benedict could hardly blame the poor woman if she was hiding from her husband. The man was almost as unpleasant as John Prescott.

Across the room, the Comstocks seemed to be holding a wordless conversation as they tried to decide how best to deal with this latest argument. After a few pointed glances passed between them, the Countess rose and announced in a voice almost loud enough to cover Elmstead's shouting, 'I do not know about the rest of you, but I cannot bare this tedium another minute.'

'And what do you mean to do about it, darling?' her husband asked. 'The rain is likely to start again at any moment.'

'We must have a ball,' the Countess said, with a sly smile that merited a look of surprise from her husband.

'But you do not have a ballroom,' Miss Williams the elder said, surprised. She was a pretty young girl, who had probably been regretting the lack of just such an entertainment.

'I have been to the music room,' her sister added. 'It is too small for dancing and the pianoforte is dreadfully out of tune.'

'On the contrary, my dear, we have a delightful ballroom, but it is exceptionally inconvenient,' the Countess replied. 'It is in an old portion of the house, shut off from the rooms we have been using. The best way to enter it is by walking through the garden. I have not mentioned it because I doubted that anyone would wish to dance after being soaked to the bone.'

'There is another way, of course,' the Earl added. 'But it is rather dangerous to have the guests creeping through the space between the walls like mice.'

'Then whatever are we to do?' said the first Miss Williams, obviously dismayed that an entertainment had been suggested only to be declared impossible.

The Countess looked to her husband and said, 'I was thinking we might do what we had discussed before the guests arrived.'

He smiled at her, obviously impressed. Then he rang for the butler and looked to the male guests in the room. 'Gentlemen, I suggest you remove your coats. We have work to do.'

The Comstocks led their guests, gentlemen in shirt-sleeves and ladies in rapt anticipation, to the entrance hall. The sound of Elmstead's shouting was clearer here. When the butler appeared, he was in the midst of listing his wife's transgressions from the first day of their marriage to the present.

'Chilson!' Comstock said in a voice loud enough to be heard over the ruckus. 'Send the footmen for the tools I used in the chapel. Then, please go upstairs and tell Lord Elmstead his presence is requested down here. We will need all hands to accomplish the job I have in mind.'

Benedict wondered if it was necessary to explain to their host that English gentlemen did not do work.

They had servants for that. Perhaps he might have, if Elmstead had not been so annoying. As it was, he was honestly curious as to why Comstock was tapping his way along the walls behind the stairs.

Elmstead appeared at the same time as a pair of footmen, carrying sledgehammers, metal bars and what appeared to be a mace from the Comstock family armoury.

Then Comstock found a panel that echoed hollow as he pounded on it. 'Here we are.' He passed the heaviest hammer to Elmstead, who stared at it in confusion.

'What do you wish me to do with this?'

'Strike the wall, my dear fellow,' Comstock said with a grin. 'From what we have all just heard, you have a stout set of lungs on you. But I suspect that your constitution and your temperament will be better after some exercise. Would you care to join us, Your Grace?' He passed the bar to Benedict and then took a hammer and chisel for himself.

They stared at Elmstead, who made a single, ineffectual strike at the centre of the panel as though afraid to damage the woodwork.

'Like this,' Comstock said, taking a mighty swing that cracked the moulding. Elmstead's next strike was a little better, though the hammer bounced back, nearly striking him. After a few minutes of industrious pounding his skill had increased and they had created a gap in the woodwork big enough for a crowbar. Benedict stuck his lever into the space, leaning into it with his whole body weight.

There was a tooth-aching screech of nails leaving wood and the panel swung free, revealing an open space where there should have been lathe or brickwork. On the other side of the gap, they seemed to be looking at the back side of another wooden panel.

Comstock looked to Elmstead. 'Again, please.' Then they began to pound on the next wall. The plan appeared to be successful in more ways than one. The longer he pounded, the more enthusiastic Elmstead became and the less concerned he seemed with his wife, who had crept down the stairs after him in ghostlike silence to watch what was happening.

This time, when the panel began to give way Benedict pushed forward with his shoulder, following with a kick that made the wall swing away in the rough semblance of a door. The Earl called for footmen to sweep the rubble from the path and then he gestured his guests forward into the large open space beyond.

'Amazing,' Mrs Prescott said, staring up at the room that had been revealed. They were standing in a grand ballroom, complete with musicians' gallery and high, floor-to-ceiling windows looking out on the wet garden at the back of the house. Quite beyond all logic, the end of the room appeared to be occupied by a chapel, separated from the dance floor by a Gothic arch of stone.

Benedict stared around him, both amazed and impressed. 'Was your home designed by a madman, Comstock?'

'Several of them, I should think,' the Earl replied. 'The mistakes made in the architecture hold to no one style or era and none of the most useful rooms connect to each other. But the walls are sound enough. And if we do not wish to tear it down, we were going to have to make a passage from one wing to the next.'

'And you have taken advantage of your guests to create it,' Benedict said, smiling back.

'But what shall we do for musicians?' Miss Williams said, staring up at the empty gallery.

'Do not fear. Comstock will provide,' the Countess said gleefully. 'Now go to your rooms to rest and arrive at eight, dressed for dancing. Tonight, we will have a light supper and a proper ball.'

Chapter Fifteen

Since they had not been travelling with proper ball-gowns, Abby's mother was near to tears at the thought that she might have to make do in the same dinner gown she had been wearing the previous night. In Abby's opinion, clothing was the least of their worries. She was still shocked and confused by the events of the last day and the multiple highs and lows of mood that she had been put through.

Lady Beverly was either a dangerous enemy or an exceptionally erratic ally. Though it was some comfort to realise that she had no desire to be Benedict's lover, she had proved herself able to cause more than enough trouble with her friendship than a brothel full of courtesans.

Benedict had been, by turns, passionate, negligent and courteous and she was still unsure which of his manners had been the truth. But of one thing she was certain: her heart had fluttered alarmingly at the sight of him in shirtsleeves breaking down walls. No matter what his intentions were, she doubted that she could resist him, should he come to her again.

Just as her mother despaired of her appearance being worthy of the Comstock ballroom, the Countess's maid appeared with gowns and headdresses from her own wardrobe.

When they went downstairs at eight, they were as elegant as the guests who had packed for the occasion.

The Comstock servants had done the house proud in preparing the ballroom on very short notice. The crystal chandeliers were fully lit. But they were no match for the cavernous space and had been supplemented by sconces and candelabras until the gilded borders along the ceiling glowed, the light flickering on the marble pillars that surrounded the room.

But on the far side of the room was the bizarre sight of the chapel fully lit. The stained-glass windows cast jewelled patterns on the floor. But to do so, they could not face out on the dark garden outside. Then Abby remembered the hidden route to the glass house and imagined the similar passages that must surround the little church and the candles that created the magical display.

'Beautiful.'

Abby turned to find Benedict standing behind her. Though he pretended to stare at the lit chapel, there was a glint in his eye that announced he had not been admiring the architecture at all.

When the rest of the guests had gathered, all equally in awe of their surroundings, the Countess announced, 'You are about to be treated to an entertainment available in no other house in England. Tonight, Comstock will be entertaining you with his banjo and teaching us some of his American dances.'

She began arranging the crowd into groups of four, assuring them, 'It is all quite simple. He thinks they are unique to his country, but they are really nothing more than English country dances.' Then she spoke louder, so her husband could hear. 'Comstock will call out the steps in badly accented French—'

'I beg your pardon?' her husband said, pretending to be shocked. 'I will speak in proper American. I cannot help it if our English forefathers did not give us enough words to make an entire language.'

'—and you have but to follow his instructions.' She finished pushing people into position, partnering couples and leading them about the room.

It did not occur to Abby until she was almost upon them that there might be a reason for Lady Comstock's enthusiasm. Before she could object, she had been placed, like the dining room silver, in a square with Lady Beverly and Benedict. A tubby baronet made the forth, glancing between her and Lenore as though terrified to partner either of them. Then he looked to Benedict with the face of a Lenten penitent.

Benedict responded with a shrug and a smile. 'It is a dance, Fellowby, not a harem. Do what Comstock tells you and try not to step on the lady's feet.'

Though Lenore looked as amused by this as the Countess, Abigail was not sure that she wanted even an oblique reference to the awkward association between three quarters of their set. Since people had been watching to see what they would do together for the last several days, this would be the topic of conversation for all of tomorrow.

But everything was forgotten as Comstock tuned his instrument, then instructed them to, 'Bow to your partner and bow to your corner.' The dance itself was not so very different from reels that she had done before. But she had never heard them set to such strange music, nor had she seen an earl serve as dancing master, plucking out tunes with surprising skill while calling strange, chanted instructions that made no sense if they had not been explained beforehand.

But the best thing about this dance was that there was no time to chat. As hours went by, they did nothing but laugh and stumble through the steps, and then laugh some more at the Earl's increasingly ridiculous instructions. When they finally stopped, the servants served a buffet of salmon and champagne followed by moulded ices and lemon tarts.

As they set their plates aside, someone called, 'Comstock! Are you capable of playing a waltz on that beastly instrument?'

Though the words had come from beside her, it took Abby a moment to recognise the voice. Perhaps it was because she had never heard Benedict speak louder than a sitting-room drawl. Nor had he ever sounded quite so joyful. When she glanced over at him, she was surprised to see him grinning from ear to ear.

'I suppose I could manage,' the Earl said, smiling back at him, tuning his strings and plucking out 'Drink to Me Only with Thine Eyes'.

Then Benedict tapped her on the shoulder and bowed deeply. 'May I have this dance, Miss Prescott?'

For a moment she stood there, mouth open, unable to form an answer. 'We have been dancing together all evening,' she reminded him. 'You are supposed to pick a new partner.'

'There are no such rules here. Now answer me quickly, or someone else will try to take you away from me,' he said. 'I see several men coming across the room for you.'

She started to turn around to see if he was telling the truth. But before she could, he had taken her hand in his, scooped the other around her waist and was swinging her into the first turn of the dance.

'I thought we agreed to be careful about drawing attention to ourselves,' she said.

'Dancing with you will do nothing to jeopardise your reputation,' he said, still smiling. 'Even if it is a dance that is not allowed at Almack's.'

'It is not too scandalous,' she said. 'I have waltzed before.'

'I am aware of that,' he said. 'You do it very nicely.' He spun her again.

'And you as well,' she replied.

'It bodes well for the future, I think. It is proof that we suit.' He smiled down at her. 'And now you are blushing. I mean that it is proof that you trust me enough to follow where I lead.'

'Oh,' she said, quietly.

'If you will allow me to lead, the next time we are together,' he added.

This made her blush even redder.

And he laughed. It was so unexpected that it startled her out of step.

'Are you attempting to prove me wrong?' he asked, giving her hand a squeeze.

'I just realised, you are talking to me,' she said.

'I am aware of the fact,' he said. 'I have done so before, you know.'

'Of course. But not when people can see us,' she said. 'Tonight, you are different. I have never seen you so relaxed in my presence.' Even in the conservatory, there had been a certain reserve as he had spoken. It was only when they had stopped talking that he had truly relaxed.

But now it almost seemed he might be blushing. Or perhaps the exertion of dancing had put colour in his cheeks. 'It takes me a while to grow used to the company of others. Lenore says I do not make sufficient effort. Usually I prefer to keep my own company. But you, Miss Prescott, are very easy to talk to.'

'Then I shall consider myself honoured to have your confidence,' she said. The words between them were polite and distant. Nothing had been said that would be inappropriate to share with strangers. Yet, if he had climbed up to the musician's gallery and shouted his love for her, it could not have been more exciting.

The dance was ending and he led her carefully to the side of the floor as Comstock was persuaded to try a gavotte. They changed partners. And though they did not stand up with each other for the rest of the evening, it did not matter. They had never been closer and she had never been happier.

Chapter Sixteen

When they retired, even though it was well past two, her mother remained in her room for nearly an hour, chattering excitedly and reliving each moment of the evening's entertainment. The night had been a true novelty for her. Since all her London invitations had included her husband, there had not been an evening for years that had not been spoiled in some way by the presence of Father. Abby reminded herself to offer Lady Comstock a special thank you before they departed for making the woman so happy.

At last, her mother returned to her own room, leaving Abby alone with her dangerous thoughts. Though the dancing had ended long ago, she felt as if she was still spinning, waltzing around the room in Benedict's arms.

It was his smile that had undone her. It was not the first time that he had lowered his guard. The moments in the conservatory had been particularly sweet, when he had lost the last of his control and gone to a place beyond normal pleasure.

But tonight, he had been not just happy, he had been joyful. It had been the same expression she had seen on him when he had been with Lenore in Bond Street. He had been chatting and talking and...

Looking at her.

She had watched the two of them together in the week they'd been here and their interactions had been pleasant enough. But he had never looked at Lenore as he had on that day in London. He had been staring at Abby through the window of the modiste's shop. And though he enjoyed talking with his friend, it had been the sight of her that had made him joyful. Even then, before they'd known each other at all, it had made him happy when he'd thought of marrying her.

Everything might have been different if he had told her how he felt.

The maid had prepared her for bed, but sleep was impossible. She was sitting on the edge of the mattress, listening to the wind rattling against the windows and thinking of him. And it was not as she'd expected to.

Last night, though she had still been angry about Lenore's trick with the book, those feelings had paled compared to her memories of the conservatory. She remembered each detail of their time, what he had said, what he had done and how it had felt. Just thinking about it had brought a return of the feelings. They were not as intense, of course. More like a happy sigh then an eruption of ecstasy. If it should end between them after the storm ended, she would put herself to sleep each night for the rest of her life, just thinking about him.

But tonight, there was curiosity along with the desire and longing. She wanted to feel again what she had felt. More than anything, she wanted to see his smile and sit at his side. She wanted him to tell her his true feelings, to make her believe that what was happening between them was as real as she wanted it to be.

To do that, they had to be together. Before she could convince herself otherwise, she was up from bed and out the door of her room, only remembering the need for secrecy after she had closed the door behind her. There was no one in their remote part of the hall, but if she saw someone on the way, she would claim to be going downstairs for a book.

She covered her mouth with her hand to keep from laughing. Lord knew what people would think of her now if she wanted reading material. If any of them had been to the library in daylight, they would not believe she was going back to it in darkness, for it was the most forbidding room she had ever seen.

If she ran into anyone now, she would ask them what they were doing out so late at night. If she meant to ruin her reputation with a liaison, then she would be as brazen about it as Lenore. That woman might be steeped in sin, but she was at least pleased about it.

The main hallway was empty in both directions, so she ran the last few yards to Benedict's bedroom, pulling the door open and darting inside without bothering to knock, then shutting it quickly and quietly behind her.

Before she could turn again, Benedict had seized her by the shoulders and spun her in his arms. 'You should not be here.' The words should have been a scold, but the expression on his face was welcoming, spreading into an easy smile as he bent and kissed her until she was breathless. He was wearing a dressing gown, but by the feel of his bare chest pressed to her, and the familiar hardness between his legs, there was nothing beneath it.

'I could not stay away,' she said when he released her.

'I am glad.' He reached for her again and she danced out of his grasp, running behind the bench at the end of the bed to put space between them.

He made a playful grab for her, ending in an exaggerated failure, his arms closing on the empty air, grinning all the time. The Duke of Danforth was teasing her, ready to chase her round the bed as if the taking of her maidenhead was some bawdy game.

And the most surprising thing about it was that she liked it. She wanted to run, but not too quickly, for she did not know what she would do if he did not catch her soon. 'I need to ask you a question,' she said, keeping the length of the bench between them as he started to circle.

He paused, disappointed. 'You came to talk.'

She shrugged. 'And...for other reasons, as well.'

'Oh.' He gave her an encouraging nod.

'But first, I need to know something.'

He sat down on the bench, patting the place beside him. Then he remained silent as she took her seat, waiting for her to speak.

'When we were in London, did you feel about me as you do now?'

He thought for a moment. 'I was not sure. But I thought I might.'

He was hesitant, falling into a lifetime of careful reserve and slipping away from her again. She tried another way. 'Tonight, when we danced… I liked it very much.'

'Thank you,' he said. It was a very proper response and very different from the man who had been ready to chase her around the room a moment ago.

'And the things we did in the conservatory. I liked them as well,' she said, watching his reaction.

The smile that had disappeared began to return. 'And if we were to do even more than that?'

Now she lost her nerve, staring down at their hands and the way their fingers twined together. 'I would like that best of all.'

He leaned towards her until his lips could brush her ear. 'I will see that you do.' He reached for her and turned her face towards his for a kiss. Then he was undoing the buttons of her nightdress and his hand slipped inside, covering her breast, massaging it until the nipple grew hard.

She turned her face away again and pressed her own hand to her chest, trapping his to still it. 'Is it proper for me to want to do what we are about to do?'

The tip of his tongue traced the shell of her ear, then his teeth closed on the lobe, making every inch of her burn with longing. 'What we will be doing is right. But if we are not married? No, it is not proper.'

He bit her ear again and, for a moment, she forgot why it mattered. Before he stopped kissing her, his lips traced the cord of her throat all the way to the shoulder. The sensation coursed in her blood and she arched her back, offering herself to him.

When he felt her submit, he pushed her back against the bedpost behind them and spread the gown wide, baring both breasts and lowering his head to take them.

She gulped a breath, trying to remember what it was that she needed to know. 'Why did we not do this in London, when you said you wanted to?'

He sighed and looked up. 'First, it was necessary to speak to your father, then to propose and to wait for the reading of the banns.'

'We would have had three whole weeks to be together,' she reminded him. 'We would have found a way.'

'I did not know you then, as I know you now,' he said.

'We have been here for little more than three days,' she countered.

'And it has been an eternity,' he said. 'It was difficult to be alone with you in London. But here, we have nothing but privacy and I can no longer control myself.'

'Nor can I,' she admitted.

He kissed her mouth again. This time, it was slower, deeper, and he did not release her until her lips felt swollen. 'No one will interrupt us here,' he whispered, reaching for the hem of her gown. 'They would not dare.'

Her hand tightened involuntarily, pressing his hand against her breast, and he took it as an invitation to squeeze while his other hand moved gently up her thigh. They were alone for as long as she wished to remain with him. And, knowing what had occurred in the brief time she had spent with him, she was both frightened and excited by what might happen tonight.

But before it did, she had to be sure of him.

'Wait.'

It was a sign of his excellent control that he listened to her, his hands going slack. 'You are not ready?'

'You have not... I do not know...' She stumbled over the words. Even though his mouth was not on her, the knowledge that it was inches from her skin made every part of her body long for his kiss. 'What...?' She gasped. 'What happens afterwards?'

Now, he stopped, surprised. 'I thought that was understood.'

She laughed. Or at least, she tried to. The sound came out as something between a sigh and a squeak. Then she took a deep breath and pushed his hands away. 'You have said nothing, Your Grace. You have given me no assurance. You have made no promises to me. Before I give myself to you, I need to know what will happen tomorrow.'

'I have done it again, haven't I?' he said, leaning back just far enough to allow her sanity to return. 'Making assumptions about your understanding of my motives?' Keeping his hands away from her, he leaned in and gave her a quick kiss on the jawline, then tucked a lock of her hair behind her ear so he could look into her eyes.

For a moment, her resolve failed. Suppose she had

pushed too hard? Suppose he thought the better of what they had been doing and was about to send her back to her room? She moved towards him again, opening her mouth for another kiss.

He placed his hands on her shoulders and held her away. 'I cannot do what I need to, if you look at me in that way,' he said. His eyes were averted, but there was a smile playing on his lips. 'I cannot think and speak. All I want to do is act.'

The grip on her shoulders lingered for a moment and he sighed, as if gaining strength. Then, one hand trailed down her arm to take her fingers, touching them lightly to his lips as he dropped to one knee. 'Miss Abigail Prescott, I love you as I have never loved a woman before. Will you do me the honour of giving me your heart to keep and your hand in marriage?'

This proposal was as different from the last one as the moon was from the sun. Yet it was still not quite what she had expected. Though she did not doubt that he was sincere, there was a formality to it, as though he had found the perfect words in a book and was reciting them to her. But he had said that he loved her and he had sworn that he never lied.

'Yes,' she said, laughing in relief that he had finally said the one word she had needed to hear. 'Yes.'

He let out a sigh of his own, as if he had feared that she might refuse him. 'At last,' he said. 'Finally.' Then he looked up at her with a sly smile and his hands were on her thighs, easing her legs apart.

She resisted, confused. They were not even in the bed yet and he was still on the floor before her. She was not totally sure what was happening, but she was certain that it had not been part of her mother's explanation.

'Since I am on my knees before you, I am in the perfect position to beg. But I hope that you will allow me to retain my honour and will give me freely what I want.' He was smiling again and far more glib now that there was a goal in sight.

A delicious shiver ran down her spine, settling near to the place where his hands touched her. She relaxed, closing her eyes.

'You will not be sorry,' he said, in a soft tone that made her insides melt. She felt a chill as he bunched her gown at her waist and then the heat of his mouth on the skin of her leg.

He kissed her between the legs, just as he had on the mouth. His tongue swirled, darted and drew secret patterns like the sigil of some magic spell. And it must have been magic, for the pleasure was unlike anything she'd felt. She broke for him almost instantly, crying his name, then swallowing the sound as she realised that someone might hear it.

He chuckled against her thigh, then rose and scooped her off the bench, carrying her to the bed. 'Velvet hangings, my love. Thick walls as well. Do not be afraid to tell me what you feel.'

'Benedict?' she said, as he pulled back the covers and tossed her into the middle of it.

He let out a happy sigh. 'If you wish to cool my blood, then call me Danforth. But do not think you can use my given name to get me to stop.'

'Benedict,' she repeated. 'I do not want to stop. But will we be married very soon?'

'Whenever you like.' He reached for her, pulling her nightdress up and over her head, leaving her naked. Then he undid the sash and stepped out of his dressing gown, letting it fall to the floor. 'I will swim to the village to get the vicar, if that is what you require of me.' Then he stared down at her, dazed. 'But not right now.'

'Tomorrow,' she agreed, staring in fascination at the muscles of his stomach.

He climbed into the bed. 'We will discuss it later.' He stroked her calves, then her thighs, slowly spreading her legs until he could kneel between them.

She stared down at his manhood, erect and ready for her, and felt an answering pull from her own body. He was bending her knees now, grasping her hips and tipping them to leave her exposed, open to his touch. He was staring down, as he played with the places that were still exquisitely sensitive and wet from his kisses. Then he leaned forward to touch the tip of himself to the opening of her body.

As it had been before, the feeling took her and she clutched him to her, trying to steady herself against the reaction. But this time, he would not let her come back to earth. Instead, he touched her again, taking her to even greater heights. 'Do you trust me?' he murmured the words against her skin.

'Yes,' she answered.

His fingers were inside her, spreading her. 'Then remember that I love you. More than I have ever loved. More than I ever will love. I am yours. I have been so since the first moment I saw you. And now I mean to make you mine.'

His hand withdrew and he leaned forward, and with his advance came pain.

She sucked her breath in through her teeth, fisting her hands in the sheets, repeating his words in her head. *I love you. I love you.*

'I am sorry,' he groaned. 'It will pass.'

How could he possibly know that? The pain was still there. She wanted to argue with him, to tell him that this could not possibly work.

Then he was fully inside her, his weight resting on his hands, which were placed near her shoulders on the mattress. He waited there, unmoving as she caught her breath. And slowly, she grew sure that he was exactly where he was supposed to be, joined with her, body and soul.

She shifted her hips, trying to get more comfortable.

Now it was he who groaned. He was too still. She wanted him to move, but he was waiting for her permission to act.

She released her grip on the bedclothes and reached up to touch him, running her hands down the bare skin of his sides, feeling the ribs beneath the skin.

In response, his hips gave an involuntary buck, and, to her surprise, the movement felt good. Then he stilled again with a contented sigh as if it was enough just to be with her.

But it was not enough for her. She gripped him tighter, tracing his ribs with her nails. He gave one, sudden thrust that made her back arch, then eased out of her until only the tip of him remained. This was followed by another slow slide and retreat.

He smiled down at her and leaned in to steal a kiss, pausing just before he touched her lips, forcing her to rise and meet him. The movement brought its own sort of pleasure for both of them and he rewarded her with another thrust that left her hungry for more.

Though the distance between them was only inches, it felt like miles. She put her hands on his face and pulled him down on top of her and into a deep kiss, taking his tongue into her mouth and holding it, just as she sheathed his body.

He kissed her back, eagerly, his hands cupping her breasts, teasing her nipples as his hips moved against hers. But better than that, she felt the hair of his chest against hers, the muscles of his abdomen against her belly, the delicious feel of his strong thighs between hers.

She raked his back with her nails, then stroked his flanks, digging her fingers into the rounded flesh of his hips. He was a marvel, just as she had suspected from the first moment she'd met him. She lifted her hips, timed them to his thrusts, trying to find the rhythm as her nerves tingled and her muscles tightened.

He groaned as he had in the conservatory and she felt the change in his body as he neared his release. She imagined what she had seen happening deep inside her body and tightened her muscles, ready to trap the rush of his seed. That small effort was all it took to push her over the edge, her body caressing his with wave after wave of ecstasy.

He felt it as well and gave himself up to her, her name on his lips. Then she felt the full weight of his body for the first time. What she had thought would be uncomfortably heavy was like a final embrace, warm and encompassing as the last of the passion trembled out of the pair of them. He whispered, 'Did you enjoy that?'

'No one told me that sin was so pleasant,' she said, staring over his shoulder and smiling up at the canopy of the bed.

His head dipped to nuzzle her neck. 'It is not sinning when you lie with your husband.'

'But you are not my husband,' she said, sighing as his teeth grazed her throat.

'When the storm clears, we will go straight back to London,' he said, giving her a quick kiss on the lips.

'A few moments ago, you promised you would swim for a vicar,' she reminded him. 'And there is a perfectly charming chapel, just downstairs.'

He rolled, pulling her with him until she was on top, draped across his body. 'You must learn not to listen to the words of a man who is staring at a naked goddess and minutes from paradise. We do not think clearly.'

She scrambled off him, sitting up. 'What you said was a lie?'

'Not a lie,' he assured her in a voice that was annoyingly rational. 'I will try to get to the village at dawn, if that is truly what you want.' But he said it in a way that said, if she was smart, she would not want such a foolish thing at all.

'Why would we wait?' she asked.

'What will we tell the others?' he asked, holding his

arms out to welcome her back. 'If I rush to marry you tomorrow morning, they will guess the reason for it.'

'I had not thought of that,' she said, feeling the familiar unease in her head and body edging out the pleasure she'd felt.

'And Lenore has requested a few more days, before we make any such announcement,' he added.

She felt the last of her optimism deflate. 'I am sorry that what we have just shared is inconvenient for her. Perhaps I should have asked a few more questions before I let you take me to bed. When, precisely, will my needs take priority over hers?'

'They do already,' he said, sitting up to lean against the headboard and face her.

'Then you can prove it to me by making a public break with her, tomorrow,' she said.

He frowned. 'You expect me to end my friendship with her?'

'Of course not,' she replied. 'But for my sake, you will have to end this pretend affair you have been having.'

His frown changed to the polite, faintly mocking smile he wore so often when she saw him in public. 'You will have to explain to me just how I end something that has never existed.'

'Make up a story,' she said. 'Tell the men here that you are casting her off.'

'You want me to lie?' And with that, her Benedict disappeared, leaving her alone in bed with the inaccessible Duke of Danforth.

'I want you to do something that will ensure the

rest of the world understands that you mean to take our marriage seriously,' she said.

'I have been endeavouring to prove to you that I am serious,' he replied. 'What other people think does not matter to me.'

'It matters to me,' she blurted.

'After we are married, you will learn to put it behind you,' he said.

'How?' she said, the last traces of the bliss she'd felt disappearing beneath a familiar, rising panic.

'When you are a duchess, you will find that people talk, whether they have anything to say or not. If we do not give them a scandal, they will make their own. To this end, it does not pay to be overly conscious of the tittle-tattle of nobodies.'

'I understand more than enough about gossip,' she snapped. 'All of London talks behind their hand about my mother and father. Until I met you, I was of tertiary interest to them.'

'And you handle yourself well,' he said, with an approving nod. 'I watched you in Almack's.'

'And saw what you wanted to see,' she replied. 'I was not in control, that night, I was terrified.'

'You did not look it,' he said.

'And you do not look like a man in love,' she said. 'My father's rages push me to megrims and nausea. It has only become worse, now that people stare at me wherever I go. And that is because of you and your friend Lenore.'

'I had no idea.' He was studying her, as if he expected that the solution to her problem would be written on her face.

'That night in Almack's, I feared that I would faint on the dance floor. I warned him of it and he left me alone. He knows how I get.'

'And I did not.' Was that regret, she heard? Had he finally realised the mistake he'd made?

'Then you must see that it will be impossible for me to manage if you do not explain that there is nothing between you and Lenore.'

'There is nothing to explain,' he said. 'I will spend less time with her. And if you are not travelling with me and I should chance to see her at a house party, we will make sure that our rooms are on opposite sides of the house.'

'When I am not with you?' she said.

'We will not be with each other every minute of the day,' he said. 'You will have to trust me.'

'It is not about my trust for you,' she said, feeling her head begin to ache. 'You are right that I cannot spend each moment with you. But every time we are apart, the rumours will begin again.'

'You will grow used to the nonsense in time,' he assured her.

'I do not want to grow used to it,' she said, trying not to panic. 'I cannot live like that, now, any more than I could when you first asked me to marry you.' She scrambled out of the bed and grabbed for her nightgown. 'The day of the wedding, I was too sick at the thought of marrying you to leave my room.'

'If the prospect of marriage to me made you sick, it

would have been wise to tell me before we lay together and not after.' He was right. But she had tricked herself into thinking that there would be only Benedict to love and care for her. She had forgotten that he was also the Duke, who would not talk with her, would not change for her and was now staring at her as if she was the biggest fool in England.

'I thought you had changed,' she said at last.

'And I thought you were something that you are not,' he replied. It might have hurt less if he'd sounded disappointed by the discovery. Instead, as he had in London, their conversation seemed to have no effect on him at all.

'But apparently, we are both just the same as we were,' she said. As the truth became clear, the terror in her passed and her head cleared, just as it had on their wedding day. 'We did not suit then and we do not suit now.'

She turned away from him and walked to the door, her head held high. And then, she left him. If she had been hoping for an apology, or even a plea that would delay the end, she was sorely disappointed.

Chapter Seventeen

'Gibbs!'

Benedict took a deep breath to regain his composure as the valet hustled out of the dressing room attached to the Tudor bedroom in a panic at this unusual display of temper. The current Duke of Danforth did not shout at his servants, or at anyone else, for that matter. Nor was he in the habit of swearing aloud at the weather, since only a fool vented his anger at a natural phenomenon that could not hear, or care, or change because of one man's opinion.

But then, he was quite sure he'd never had his heart broken before. Today was a day of firsts.

Though he dared not show it, when Gibbs caught sight of his clothing, that man had reason to be angry as well. 'What on earth has happened, Your Grace?'

'I went for a walk.' His tone still sounded rude, so he paused to breathe again. It was not fair of him to shout at a loyal servant for his own stupid mistake, especially when it had created so much extra work for the fellow. 'I felt the need of some air.'

It was not exactly an untruth. He had hoped that the fresh air in the very brief lull between interminable storms would help him recover some equilibrium after the previous night. Though the jilting at the church had been painful, it had been like a gnat bite compared to what he was feeling now. In London, it had been possible to take comfort in the sympathy of others. But today, he did not dare complain that the love of his life had refused his offer after giving him the ultimate prize. The most logical response of others would be to treat him as a seducer of innocents and her as the injured party who was refusing to marry a man who dishonoured her.

And poor Gibbs was still staring at him, waiting for some logical explanation as to why he had walked bareheaded into a storm. Benedict stared back at him, daring him to find anything unusual about it. 'I thought, perhaps, it might be possible to make my way to the village.' A part of him had wanted to retrieve the damned parson he had promised her. But the rest of him had wanted to walk until his mood improved and to keep walking all the way to London, if necessary, to avoid having to see Abby Prescott ever again.

But his prodigious anger had been no match for the destruction left by the recent storms and he had barely made it to the end of the drive. 'I fear I have ruined my boots. And the breeches as well.'

The valet sniffed in disapproval, but said, 'It is only mud.'

'But rather a lot of it, I am afraid.' Benedict looked down at the sad state of his clothing, which was wet through even though he had taken the time to grab an oilcloth duster to protect it. He had left that with a footman at the front door when he had returned to the house. But he suspected, had he bothered to look behind him as he'd returned to his room, he'd have seen a team of servants mopping the trail of muddy footprints and rain water that he had tracked from the entrance hall to his bedchamber. 'I thought perhaps the rain had stopped long enough for the roads to begin to dry.' He had hoped to find a coach at the nearest inn. Perhaps it was cowardly to want to run away. But for the first time in his life, he was not sure he could trust his temper to withstand another confrontation with Abby.

'It was only a temporary respite,' his valet remarked, glancing out the window at the sheets of water that were again running down the panes.

'The roads were nothing but mud.' Gibbs only had to look at the marks on his breeches to estimate the depth that Benedict discovered when sinking into a rut by the stable. 'A groom had to pull me free. I very nearly left a Hessian in a puddle.'

Gibbs stripped him of his coat and shirt and pushed him down into a chair so he could remove the offending boots. 'A few hours drying by the fire and a good brushing and they will be almost as good as new.'

Almost. That proved how dire his damage had been, for his valet did not usually admit to even a possibility that his work would not be perfect. Perhaps it was time to accept that some things might be wonderful for a time, but once broken, they could never be fixed. 'Do your best,' he said, staring down at the second thing he had ruined this week.

'We are all frustrated by the need to remain indoors for so long uninterrupted,' Gibbs said. 'But I recommend, Your Grace, that you be patient until we are sure that the weather has turned.'

This was very near to a lecture on his foolish behaviour and he was having none of that. 'I am quite capable of making my own decisions on such matters,' he said. 'And if I choose to stand in a thunderstorm and have God strike me dead, I will need nothing more from you than to polish the boots on my corpse. Do I make myself clear, Gibbs?'

'Your Grace!' The exclamation was one part apology for overstepping himself and two parts shock that his normally reasonable master had treated him in such a way.

But now that he had started being unreasonable, Benedict was in no mood to stop. 'Now get me out of these wet clothes,' he said, not bothering to hide his impatience. 'If I am trapped in this damned house with these damned people, you had damned well better see that I look my best when I go downstairs.'

In less than an hour, Gibbs had helped him into fresh linen and a pressed coat and he'd been shaved, perfumed, curried and combed like someone's prized mare. Despite the fact that it was exactly what he'd asked for, Benedict had had to resist the urge to bat away the normally soothing hands of his valet and demand he be left in peace and looking like the wreck he felt. Though the service was in no way different than what had been done to him for decades, today the fussing made him feel he was as incapable of caring for himself as he was in managing his own romantic life.

How could he have not realised that the only woman he had ever loved was unable to navigate the future he'd planned for her.

It was even more annoying to come downstairs and see Abby Prescott seeming so well now that she was rid of him. He paused in the doorway of the salon, pretending to survey the room, but his attention was only for her. Though she'd been up half the night with him, she looked rested and, worse yet, content. He had thought she'd have had the decency to be distraught by the end of their second engagement. If she had truly cared at all for him, she should be languishing for his loss.

Instead, she looked even lovelier than before. Could it be that their lovemaking had evoked a change in her appearance? She seemed almost luminous in the late morning light. Or was it simply that knowing he could never have her again made her more beautiful to his eyes? Her maid had dressed her hair in a casual style, leaving a single curl dangling against the left side of her face. It made him long to brush it back, to see if it would raise a blush on her cheek.

'Your Grace!' Her mother waved to him and smiled, eager to be the first one he spoke to. Perhaps she was remembering how happy he had looked as he'd danced with her daughter only the night before and hoping to see they were about to announce the end of their difficulties.

'Mrs Prescott,' he said, bowing in acknowledgment. 'Miss Prescott.' He was sure his smile looked more like a grimace, but he was no longer capable of treating her with his best society manners.

Abby said nothing in return, but looked back at him with the smile of a Madonna in an oil painting. She was unspeakably lovely and totally serene, but unmoved by the one gazing on her. Or perhaps she was Eve. The blushes from the day before had disappeared, as if all it had taken to give her womanly composure was one last scrap of forbidden knowledge.

'Did you sleep well?' Her mother remained unaware of the tension between them and was eager to converse.

'Sleep? No. Not a wink.' He had not intended to display such weakness in front of the woman who had caused it, but neither did he mean to let her escape what she had done to him. She deserved to suffer, if only vicariously.

'Tonight, you must have the maids prepare you some hot milk before bed.' Mrs Prescott was rambling in the background as he stared at her daughter. 'Or perhaps the Countess has some herbal concoction that might do just as well.'

'I will ask her,' he replied, ready to say anything that would end the small talk and allow him to go to a corner to lick his wounds. Before she could think of another comment to hold him, he turned away from her, not bothering to excuse himself. But he was barely out of earshot before he was stopped by Lenore.

'You look like death warmed over,' she said, with a smile of approval over the reason she'd assumed for his sleeplessness.

'Thank you for your opinion,' he said, not bothering to hide his annoyance. 'In the future, please keep it to yourself.'

She stared at him, eyebrows raised in shock. 'I do not think I have ever heard you take that tone with me in the whole of our acquaintance.'

'Then I suggest you grow used to it,' he said. 'You will be hearing much more of it in the future.'

Now her brows knit in confusion and her eyes registered something very like hurt. 'If you are having trouble with…' She stopped before she could say the name that they were both thinking in a room where anyone might overhear. 'If it is someone else that is bothering you, I do not see why you feel the need to take your anger out on me.'

Who else could he punish, other than himself? If he could not manage to be civil, he did not dare to speak to Abby again on that or any other subject. Everything that had happened between them must be consigned to the deepest dungeon of his soul where it could never again see the light of day. It was not enough that it would brand him a rake for ever. Even a hint of it would ruin her, leaving her fair game to any man who valued his own pleasure more than a woman's honour. Worse yet, now that he knew how it hurt her, he could not bring himself to cause any more gossip.

He stared back at Lenore, suddenly sick of the sight of her. 'I am abusing you because you should share the blame for my unhappiness,' he said. 'If I had cut you from my life a year ago, I would be happily married by now.'

'I have done nothing objectionable to you or with you,' she insisted. 'I told her so. She believed me, I swear.'

'And now are you willing to tell everyone else?' he said. 'Because the woman I love cannot live in the shadow of our supposed affair. And after ten years, it would be far easier to prove a positive than a negative.'

'I...can't.'

Of course she couldn't. Society would not stand for the truth. It was unreasonable of him to suggest it, especially when it had been his idea to use their friendship to protect her. It was quite possible that he was ending his oldest friendship with that rudeness. But he could not manage to care.

If he could not have Abby, then there was no future for him. Why would he care about the past? 'Then I have no use for you,' he said, turning away from her just as he had from the Prescotts, strangely satisfied by the murmurs from people around him who had witnessed their argument.

He turned towards the sound and it stopped immediately. Then he swept the room with a gaze that assured there would be no more gossip. There was an unfamiliar thrill at feeling their fear of him. It was much more satisfying than the usual cautious courtesy he felt when people wondered about him.

In the silence he'd created, he walked to a chair in the corner and picked up the newspaper that someone had left lying on it, then unfolded it and began to read. It was a week old, at least, and he had read the articles in it that interested him several days ago. But until he could find a way to excuse himself from this stultifying group, it would be an adequate bar to further conversation.

Then, just as he'd begun to get comfortable, there was another disturbance. A man was shouting in the upstairs hall.

Elmstead, arguing with his wife. Again. Annoying though he was, the man had truly impressive abilities. The sound of his voice carried from the first floor all the way to the salon. A day or two ago, Benedict had been able to ignore their arguments, since he did not involve himself in things that did not concern him. But today, it grated on his nerves. He gave his newspaper a rattle and then set it aside, giving the Countess of Comstock a warning glare to remind her that she was responsible for keeping the peace.

But she was too preoccupied with eavesdropping to pay attention to him. In fact, everyone in the room appeared to be absorbed in the drama occurring upstairs. Lady Hanover was even shameless enough to set her needlework aside and go to open the door wider, letting in as much of the entertainment as possible. Then she leaned out into the hall, so she might not miss anything.

From his corner of the room, Danforth let out a loud sigh of disgust, to remind them all how common they were being. But when he scanned the faces around him, it was clear that what was happening between the Elmsteads outweighed censure from a peer.

Only Abby appeared to be bothered by any of it. The soft smile she'd been wearing as he'd entered had disappeared, replaced by a blush of embarrassment. Considering her history, it was hard to tell whether her colouring was caused by remembered family shame or actual sympathy for Lady Elmstead. Either way, it was a reminder to him of how superior she was to the rest of his acquaintances. The memory evoked a fresh stab of emotion, both anger and regret.

'Whore!' The word exploded out of the general rumble of male shouting and feminine weeping from above, drawing a gasp of shock from the audience in the salon.

This was followed by a feminine wail and an unintelligible response that was clearly a denial, and then a sudden shriek.

Though some hesitated to involve themselves in a matter that was between husband and wife, this argument was worse than the shouting matches they'd heard thus far. Benedict shot to his feet with the involuntary need to come to the aid of a lady who was obviously in distress. Before he could take a step, the Earl of Comstock was halfway to the door, unwilling to let violence be done under his roof.

Before either of them could do anything, the door flew open the rest of the way, crashing against the wall as Elmstead appeared, one fist balled in rage and the other locked around his wife's bicep. As they crossed the threshold, she struggled free of him and rushed into the arms of the Countess of Comstock, who looked momentarily baffled before offering her a comforting pat on the back. Lenore stepped forward as well, gathering the dishevelled and tearful lady into a sisterly embrace, brushing the hair from her face and exposing her cheek which appeared to be reddening from a slap.

From the protective shelter of her arms, Lady Elmstead turned back to confront her husband. 'Stop it this instant, Gerald. Things are not at all as they appear.'

'I can see what has been going on, you stupid trollop. I am not blind.'

From the angry murmurs of the other guests, he was not only wrong, but devoid of manners. Mrs Prescott whispered something about a 'toady little man'. Though the full comment was obscured by Abby's hiss of warning to be silent, there were several nods of agreement. Though most felt it was impolite to speak the thought aloud, there was nothing she might have done that justified striking one's wife, especially when she was as young and slight as Lady Elmstead.

But from the steely glint in Lenore's eye as she stared at him, Benedict had a good guess as to the true depth of his mistake.

'Mind your temper, Elmstead. You are in the presence of ladies and gentlemen and not visiting some dockside brothel.' Any other day he might have been able to hold his tongue and allow Comstock to settle the matter. At the very least, he'd have chosen his words with care to avoid making things any worse. But today, Benedict was in no more mood for distance and diplomacy than Elmstead was.

That man was still framed in the doorway, like a comic-opera cuckold who had not been told he was the villain of the piece instead of the hero. He seemed surprised at the derision from his audience and scanned the room for the man audacious enough to challenge him. Then he stared directly at Benedict and said, 'Danforth! Of course. The one with the most to hide will always speak the loudest.'

As everyone waited for his response, the silence in the room grew ominous, punctuated by Lord Elmstead's rapid breathing and another quiet sob from his wife.

'I beg your pardon?' Though he was used to being gossiped about, Benedict could not remember a time when someone had come so close to offering a direct insult. As with so many minor social slights, it was best to pretend not to hear and give the fellow a chance to reconsider and retract. Bemusement was called for, not anger. But today Benedict made no effort to hide his irritation at being dragged into the Elmsteads' domestic problems.

'You heard me the first time,' Elmstead said. 'Do not pretend that you don't know what we are speaking of.' The words came in another roar. Between the bellowing and the florid colour of his face, the man looked like a pig in a striped-silk waistcoat. And though they had barely spoken ten words together for the whole of the week, he had decided to pick a fight.

He had been shouted at by far better men then Elmstead. He had weathered sixteen years of storms, far stronger than this. He had ignored them, clutching his fists until the nails cut the palms and grinding his teeth until his jaws ached. He'd stayed quiet for decades, until it had eaten away at his common sense and spoiled his life.

But that silence was no longer needed. Benedict responded to the pathetic little man in front of him in the way he deserved, with derisive laughter. 'Know what you are speaking of? Not a clue,' he replied. Then he thought back to the word that had shocked the room earlier. 'If you think that I have some part in your argument with your wife, then you had best think again.' It was another chance to retract and more than the fellow deserved.

'Involved with my wife? That is exactly what I think,' Elmstead shouted back.

'Then you should go back to your room and sober up,' Benedict snapped, wondering what had got into the man. 'But before you do, apologise to your wife and the rest of the guests for your beastly behaviour.' *And to me as well.* He did not bother to add a thing that should be obvious to any sensible person.

'You deny that you are her lover?'

This brought another gasp from the room. There was no way to pretend a misunderstanding or deny that he had heard it, nor could he contain the rage building inside at such abuse from such a common little man. 'Of course, I deny it and I expect you to withdraw the insult immediately. I have no idea what gave you such a ridiculous idea.'

'This! Yours. Found in my wife's bedroom.' Elmstead took the final step across the room and threw a handkerchief into the Duke's face. Rather, he tried, for the linen square had no weight to do any kind of damage as a projectile. As it fluttered to the ground, Benedict could see his own family crest embroidered in the corner.

'Elmstead, have a care.' This came from Lord Comstock, attempting to calm the storm. On the other side of the room, Lady Comstock had taken Lady Elmstead's hand and was leading her out into the hall, away from the public discussion of her behaviour.

'You found that in your wife's room?' For a moment, his mind went utterly blank. He was unable to explain the presence of the handkerchief, even if he'd wanted to. The only thing he was sure of was that it had not been the result of some clandestine romance with Lady Elmstead.

'Where you left it,' Lord Elmstead bellowed back, probably still assuming that Benedict would blurt out a confession if he shouted loud enough.

But he still had nothing to admit.

Then he remembered the maid and her pearls. She had been searching for silk, asking the other maids for help. Had she said Elmstead? If so, there was a perfectly logical reason that his lost linen had ended up on the wrong bedside dresser. Though Lady Elmstead might be guilty of something, she would have had no way to explain its presence.

He could announce the truth, should he wish to. But as Comstock had pointed out when he had explained it to him, it sounded far less believable than the things people had assumed about his behaviour. He did not want to jeopardise the maid's position any more than he had on the day it had happened. Nor was he going to tell anyone that he had an alibi for last night, as he had not been alone for any part of it, until Abby Prescott had spurned him for the second time.

The wisest course of action was to tell Elmstead that he had never been anywhere near the lady, or her room. But he had left wisdom behind some time after he'd opened his bedroom door and was not in the mood to take it back. Instead, he sneered and said, 'Have we decided to perform *Othello* to pass the time? You are making a public scene over a scrap of cloth that I misplaced days ago.'

'Liar!' Elmstead cried.

'Apologise now, or you will regret those words.' Now he was beyond anger, into something that felt far more dangerous and his voice sounded like the tone his own father used, right before things became unbearable.

'The time for words is past,' Elmstead shouted back, ignoring the warning. Then his hand came up, almost from the ground, and landed a blow on Benedict's chin that sent him staggering to his knees.

Like most gentlemen of his set, Benedict had sparred at Gentleman Jackson's salon. But it took a blow from an angry husband to show him just how gently the professional pugilist had treated him. One punch from Elmstead and his head was ringing, he tasted blood and one of his molars felt loose.

Something else was loose, as well. The inside of his brain felt as if a cage door had been unlocked and the monster he'd kept there had been released. He had thought that rage would be an emotion of heat. But what he was feeling now was the ice-cold certainty that no man who struck the Duke of Danforth would live to do it again.

He shook off Comstock's offer of aid as he rose, only vaguely aware of the deathly silence of the room around him. The guests were watching like so many jackals at a kill, waiting for their share of gore.

And though he knew better than to do so, he could not seem to keep himself from looking at Abby. Unlike the others, she stared at him, white-faced and trembling, as though she feared for his safety. Or perhaps it was Elmstead she worried about, for as he stared at her, she mouthed the single word, *No.*

If she cared at all about him, she was a day too late to show it.

He could feel blood trickling from the corner of his mouth, so he bent down and snatched up the handkerchief that Elmstead had thrown at his feet, wiped his split lip and then tossed the red-stained rag back at his adversary's feet. Then he did not so much speak, as roar, 'Find a second, Elmstead. We meet at dawn.'

Chapter Eighteen

'Head back. Eyes open.'

Benedict felt like an idiot. But he lifted his chin, obediently, and waited as Comstock took a candle from the library table and passed it before his eyes, then ran a finger down his nose, feeling for breaks.

'Got me square on the jaw,' Benedict muttered, wishing he could blame a brain injury for what had happened next. Though the blow had been more than enough to daze him, he had been in full command of his faculties when he had issued the challenge.

'Your eyes are clear. But he drew claret, as you English like to say.'

'You are English,' Benedict reminded him, running his hand along the bruised flesh and wincing.

'As of late, I am,' the Earl agreed with a shrug, then handed him a fresh handkerchief to mop the blood from his chin and a glass of harsh American whiskey to numb the pain of the bruise blossoming on his jaw. 'I didn't think Elmstead had the pluck to punch you.'

'I didn't deserve it,' Benedict muttered, annoyed at the slurring of the words through his swollen lip.

'All the same, it would have been wiser to wait until he calmed down to explain that.'

The Earl was right. He had never responded with anger to the things people assumed about him. He knew better than to settle problems with violence, especially when in another man's home. He was the one who gave such advice instead of receiving it. He had done so just last night with Abby. But in the few hours since he had lost her, the emotions that he'd kept properly bottled for decades had come spilling out without warning. Today, it had been as if his father had been alive again, speaking though him. 'I couldn't let the insult pass,' he said at last, confused by the truth of it.

Comstock's eyebrow arched. 'And yet you have allowed the *ton* to think anything it wanted to about you and your lady friend for years on end.'

'What the *ton* thinks about my relationship with Lenore does not concern me,' he mumbled. But his words did not sound nearly as convincing as they had a day or two ago.

'Because you are not lovers,' Comstock finished.

In ten years, Comstock was the first one to guess the truth. It was almost a relief to drop the façade. 'How did you know?'

'My Countess spotted the truth from the moment the pair of you arrived.'

'Really?' This was truly surprising, for most of the women who had learned the truth about Lenore were the ones least likely to announce it to their husbands. 'And it does not concern you?'

Comstock grinned back at him. 'Charity's interest in Lady Beverly is purely academic, though I admit that it has led to some very interesting conversations between us. But Lady Elmstead's knowledge of Lenore is another matter entirely.' Then, he grew serious. 'We both know that you were not the one with her last night.'

Benedict sighed. 'I was…elsewhere. I would rather not discuss the details.'

'Because the honour of another lady is involved,' Comstock said, with an annoying amount of certainty.

'That is not a matter I care to discuss. But I can assure you that the presence of my handkerchief in the Elmstead rooms is nothing more than a coincidence.'

Comstock gave a dismissive huff. 'It is a small scrap of fabric to base such accusations on. But I do not expect Lady Elmstead will admit to the truth, now that her husband suspects her of infidelity. She would much rather he think you were to blame than to know the truth. And the story is easily believed because of your reputation as a libertine.'

'A libertine,' Benedict said vaguely. In the depths of his mind, his father's voice announced that someone should remind this upstart American that a glass of whiskey and a house-party invitation did not entitle him to lecture his betters. But he was able to dismiss the thought without too much effort. It seemed that the blow and subsequent challenge had cleared some of the fog of rage from his mind. 'A libertine?' he repeated.

'It shouldn't surprise you, Danforth,' Comstock said, not even bothering to soften the criticism with an honorific. 'From what I am told, you have been running around with the Marchioness for years. Then, out of nowhere you decided to marry the lovely Miss Prescott, who promptly threw you over. No one knows the reason, but it is commonly assumed to be some dastardly behaviour on your part. A tryst with another lady would hardly be out of the realm of possibility. And now, with this fresh scandal...'

'I never listen to gossip,' Benedict replied. Though he had been using it for years, it was a surprisingly unsatisfying answer. After today, he should not be surprised that everyone was likely to assume the worst about him in the future.

'Perhaps you should begin to pay attention,' Comstock suggested. 'If you had made any effort to protect your reputation before today, then this situation would not have happened.'

It was annoyingly logical. 'I will take it under advisement,' he said, pressing the lump of ice a maid offered him against his bruised face to prevent the reoccurrence of his newfound temper.

'For now, I would like to know your plans for tomorrow,' Comstock said, still as reasonable as if they were trying to decide on lawn tennis or croquet. 'Though the rain seems to have stopped for the day, I can offer no guarantees on what dawn might bring. Even if the skies will be dry, the fields are muddy. But as I have said before, the house is large. If you intend to duel inside, I can supply you with swords.'

Until illness had rendered his right arm useless, his father had been ready to grab a sword over the smallest offence. With such a poor example, Benedict had vowed to avoid doing any such thing. It had taken only a single lapse of judgement and he was trapped.

'Swords will be fine,' he agreed, thinking they were the lesser of two evils. A sabre cut was more easily cleaned than a pistol wound, but either could be deadly. 'It is not my place to choose,' he added.

There was a moment of silence from Comstock, as if praying for strength. 'The Code Duello. Of course. Not being a gentleman until recently, I've never had cause to read it. The challenged chooses the weapon to prevent the challenger from picking a fight, then using his strongest skill.'

Benedict nodded.

'I will apply some gentle pressure to Elmstead's second to make sure he chooses what we want him to,' Comstock said. 'And I make no claims as to the quality of the weapons. I will ask Charity to choose the best two of them, since she played with them as a child.'

'Played with swords?'

Comstock shrugged. 'The Stricklands are a most unusual family. Speaking of seconds, have you given thought to yours?'

'Seconds,' Benedict said numbly. The position should fall to his best friend. His best male friend, that was, for he could hardly expect Lenore to test weapons and negotiate for his honour. Now that he thought about it, he did not have a best male friend. He could think of damn few acquaintances that might do the job and no one at all in this party that he considered himself close to.

But Comstock had been helping him to recover from the blow and working to minimise the mess he had made in issuing a challenge at all. He looked at the Earl. 'You, I suppose.' He thought for a moment. 'If you will accept the job, that is.'

'It will be a new experience for me,' Comstock admitted. 'But I will try to do my best. I suppose it is too much to hope that you will apologise to Elmstead and end this before it begins.'

'I have nothing to apologise for,' Benedict said.

'An explanation, perhaps?'

'Several,' he admitted. 'None of which I plan to share.'

'A convincing lie?'

'I never lie,' Benedict said.

'Your relationship with Lady Beverly?'

'An omission of facts. Since I do not listen to gossip, I have no reason to correct it.'

'You draw a fine line between truth and falsehood, Your Grace,' Comstock said, with another shrug.

'Probably true,' he agreed. 'But it is there, all the same. I will not apologise for something I did not do and I doubt Elmstead is going to take my word of honour that I did not bed his wife. I am afraid I will have to go through with it.' Then he added, 'I am sorry to be spoiling your party.'

'I would not call it ruined,' Comstock allowed.

'Many of the guests are insisting that this is the most diverting week they have had all Season.'

Ghouls. Abby had been right about the vicious nature of the people around them. He had ignored her and she had been right all along. 'Then I hope I do not spoil their fun if I do not kill Elmstead,' he said, as Comstock refilled the glass in his hand. 'No matter how far this goes, I will not murder a man over a mistake.'

'And if he decides to kill you?'

It was an excellent question and one he did not yet have an answer to. As he took his first sip and considered it, there was a knock at the door.

'That will be Miss Prescott,' Comstock said with a smile. 'I suspect she will be eager to speak to you about this.'

'I would prefer to avoid that,' he said, finally recognising his duty to protect her from the public gaze now that it was too late.

'And I would prefer that my guests not draw each other's blood. It appears we are both to be disappointed today, Your Grace,' Comstock replied, finally out of patience. 'You wish me to orchestrate mayhem and conceal it afterwards to protect the combatants from the law. But I will not settle your love life for you. You must do it yourself.'

'Apologies,' he said and held his glass up in a silent toast. 'Let the lady in and send my regards to Elmstead.'

'Of course.' Comstock opened the door and, after a brief conversation, Abby entered and shut and locked it after her.

* * *

Was it a sign of how much she loved him, or simply an indication of excellent breeding that, bruised and bleeding, he was no less poised and elegant than he had been in London? He was sprawled in an armchair, glass in one hand, ice bag in the other, staring blankly out the window.

It was an improvement on his earlier mood, for Benedict had been positively belligerent since he had come down to breakfast. After years of living under the tyrannical rule of her father, she did not find him all that fearsome. Then she reminded herself that it did not matter if she could live with his moods, since she had declared herself free of him just a few hours ago.

'If you have come to tell me what an idiot I am, you needn't have bothered. Comstock has done it already.' Benedict took a sip from his glass without bothering to turn towards her. Whatever it contained was potent enough to make him wince as it touched his damaged lip.

'You are not foolish,' she said, forcing herself to remember that it was not appropriate to kiss his wounds to soothe them, when she had been partly responsible. 'You are simply too noble. All you must do is tell Elmstead what you were really doing last night. He will withdraw his accusation, apologise for the insult and the matter will be settled.'

Benedict tried to laugh and winced again. 'Put that idea out of your head this instant for it is not going to happen. Despite what you might feel about me, I…care far too much about you to do such a thing.'

Had it been her imagination, or had he been about to say he loved her? It was unreasonable to expect such a thing after the way she'd treated him, but she could not help hoping. 'If your life is in danger, what is the point of protecting something as flimsy as my reputation?'

'Do not be so melodramatic. My life is not at risk,' he said gruffly, taking another drink. 'I do not intend to let Elmstead kill me over something I did not do, nor do I mean to kill him.'

'And when you got up this morning, I doubt you meant to challenge someone to a duel,' she snapped. 'Accidents happen. Mistakes are made. You cannot predict the future and promise me that nothing will happen.'

'I did last night,' he reminded her.

'And I did not believe you,' she shot back. 'But that was another matter entirely.'

'Our future,' he said. Though his expression was as stoic as ever, the lost tenderness had returned to his voice.

'We are not talking about that,' she said. 'We are talking about right now. And I am not going to allow you to risk your life to protect my honour.'

'Then we are at an impasse,' he said, managing a gentle smile with his damaged mouth. 'I will not ruin your life to protect my own. Especially since it has been pointed out to me that you were right all along.'

'In what way?'

'I should not have ignored the rumours that were spread about me, for they were what led to this circumstance. If people thought me above reproach, then I'd never have been accused.' Then, his expression softened. 'More importantly, I would not have lost you.'

You did not lose me, she wanted to argue. *I am right here.* And yet, though she was only a few feet away from him, it felt like a distance of miles when she thought of how close they had been last night.

'You would not have lost your temper if it weren't for me either,' she reminded him.

'Do you blame yourself for your father's outbursts?' he asked.

She considered for a moment. 'No. His flaws are his own.'

'Then do not take credit for mine,' he said. 'I thought that controlling my behaviour was the same as controlling my reputation. I thought that if I could control my emotions, they would not cause me trouble. It seems I was wrong on both counts.'

'Your sudden self-awareness does little good at this point,' she said, 'if you are not willing to find a way out of this mess you have made.'

'I have a way,' he said, equally firm. 'I will meet with him at dawn. We will exchange a few passes with the sword, I will draw a small amount of blood and honour will be satisfied.'

'But if something goes wrong, you will die,' she insisted.

'Does it really matter so much if it does?' He seemed surprised.

'Of course,' she replied. 'Because I love you.'

'And yet you will not marry me,' he reminded her, his emotionless expression returning an hour too late to do them any good.

'Love and marriage have very little to do with each other,' she said. She had only to look at her parents to realise that.

'And yet, for us, I had hoped it might be different.' There was a softness in his voice as he said it, that made her want to crawl into his arms and never leave.

'It still can be,' she said, sitting on the divan beside him, so close that their legs were touching. 'If you promise me that you will go to Elmstead and call a halt to this, I will accept your proposal. We will go to the village, just as you offered last night. Or Gretna. Anywhere you wish.' Her skull throbbed at the thought of what the future might be. But if she had to, she would hide in whatever great house he took her to and never face society again. She would find a way to manage if only he were safe.

He reached out to her, covering her hands with one of his. 'Much as I appreciate the offer, I do not think it is possible to escape from the house. The least reason being that I tried to run away from you just this morning and could not manage to get to the end of the drive for all the mud.'

He had been trying to leave her. If he did not want to be with her, what did she have to offer? 'Tomorrow, then,' she said. 'We can be together.'

He shook his head. 'You cannot bribe me into crying off this duel. I was a fool to lose control when provoked, but neither can I apologise for something I did not do. Even if I could, the things you feared last night would still be present tomorrow. I have tainted our future with my carelessness, Abby, and I cannot for the life of me think of how to put it right.'

'Suit yourself, then,' she said, pulling her hands away from him. 'If you truly loved me, you would know how precious your life is to me and would be less careless with it.'

'It will be all right,' he said again. It was neither a lie nor the truth, but the statement of a man who did not know what might happen, but had grown tired of arguing about the inevitable.

Her next visit was to the room beside the Tudor bedroom, the one she was sure must belong to Lady Beverly. If that woman was surprised to find her knocking at the door, she did not show it. She simply opened it and allowed her to enter.

'Benedict is being an idiot,' Abby said, pacing the rug in front of the bed and fighting the urge to rush back downstairs to find the Earl and demand he help.

'All men are idiots over something,' Lenore replied. 'And Danforth is a fool for you. You are the reason he cannot explain himself. You know perfectly well where he was on the night in question.'

'So does Lady Elmstead,' Abby reminded her. 'She knows he was not with her. Yet I did not hear her denying the affair.'

'Her husband would not believe her if she did,' Lenore replied. 'And if he were to find out who she was really with, it might go even worse for her than another of his endless rages. Men sometimes respond with violence when they realise that their rival is a woman.'

'You,' Abby said.

Lenore nodded. 'I doubt Elmstead could call me out should she try to explain the matter. But it would be far more scandalous than duelling with a duke over her.'

'Then how else can we keep them from fighting?'

But the woman who had tricked her way through life and took great joy in thumbing her nose at convention had very little to offer. 'Elmstead shows no sign of withdrawing, since he is sure he's in the right. And you do not know Danforth very well if you think he will lie and apologise for something he did not do. Nor will he betray a confidence,' Lenore added. 'Your reputation is safe with him, whether you want it to be or not.'

'Of course,' Abby said, surprised to find that the thing she had most hoped for came at such a high price. 'And if they do fight, what might happen?'

'I doubt that anyone will die,' Lenore replied, parroting the same hope that Benedict did. 'Danforth is more than fair with a sword. He will not allow himself to be seriously injured. But he might be forced to defend himself.'

'And if Elmstead dies?'

'Duelling is illegal. And a peer can only be tried for murder in the House of Lords.' Lenore considered for a moment. 'But it would probably be easier if he decided to flee the country indefinitely.'

'Flee?'

'He might think that gossip does not matter. But the scandal will be such that he will not be welcomed in polite society. He will be blackballed from his clubs and his friends, such as they are, will turn their backs on him.'

Abby had already reconciled herself to the fact that she would not be seeing him again after the party had ended. But she had never imagined that he would not even be in the same country. 'What are we going to do?' she whispered.

'Does it really matter to you so much, what happens to him?' Lenore looked at her with surprise. 'He has given you what you want: a future free from scandal. I doubt that anyone will notice you for the rest of your stay here, nor will your names be linked afterwards. No matter the results of the duel, it will be assumed that his lover was Lady Elmstead.'

'I did not want my reputation restored at his expense,' she said. 'Or hers.'

'Then you had best get used to your success,' Lenore said, annoyed. 'I cannot think of a single thing that will not make the matter worse.'

'That has never prevented you from acting before,' Abby stated. 'He is in this mess because of your selfishness, just as much as mine. He is protecting your reputation as well. And now you mean to abandon him.'

'As if you have not,' Lenore retorted. 'You have left him twice already, you know.'

'Because I am not the one he wants,' she blurted. 'He needs someone stronger. Someone better. He needs a duchess.'

'It is a pity we do not have one here to talk sense to him,' Lenore said, eyeing her coldly. 'But I doubt he would listen to her, should the perfect woman appear. He has been yours since the first moment he laid eyes on you. You are the only one who has the power to stop this. If you cannot, tomorrow, he will be totally alone. There is nothing the rest of us can do but wait for it to be over.'

Chapter Nineteen

It was Benedict's understanding that duels were fought just after sunrise, in a field far from the prying eyes of one's friends and neighbours. But he had no actual, practical experience on the subject. Until yesterday, he had been far too sensible to be involved in one, even as a second.

It seemed that his first and last affair of honour was going to be as unusual as everything else at Comstock Manor. The Earl and Elmstead's second had walked the grounds on the previous afternoon and declared them hopeless for battle. And though the rain seemed to have stopped, short of consulting an almanac, it was difficult to judge the rising of the sun, against the perpetual mist rising from the sodden ground.

After some discussion, it had been decided that the fight would occur at six o'clock in the ballroom, where the morning light would be shining through the eastern windows. Since it was well before breakfast, the rest of the guests would still be asleep and the matter could be settled in private with little interference or interruption.

Despite the fact that the participants had been sworn to secrecy, Benedict arrived in the ballroom at half past five to find a crowd gathering along the wall, awaiting the commencement of the action. 'I was under the impression that this was a matter to be settled between gentlemen and not a spectator's sport,' he said to Comstock, who was staring with disapproval at the guests, munching their toast while the footmen carried in the swords.

'I would swear that no one spoke of it, but as with everything else in this house, news travels fast,' the Earl replied.

'There is nothing to be done, I suppose,' Benedict said, staring in disapproval at the gawkers. 'Have you found someone to stand as surgeon for us?'

'I managed to send a message to our local doctor,' Comstock said. 'But he refused to take any part in patching up men who are intent on doing each other injury. He says it only encourages foolishness.'

'Normally, I would consider that extremely good sense,' Benedict replied. 'But since it might be my hour of need, I find it hard to be so understanding.'

'I have some small knowledge of medicine,' Comstock said. 'I would advise you not to get stuck in anything vital. But I am quite handy with a needle and thread, as long as the cuts are not too deep.'

Benedict grimaced. 'It will have to do, I suppose.' Then, he added, 'It was never my intent that it should go this far.' By the looks of it, Elmstead had not wanted this either. His normally red face was pale in the morning light, his volatile manner quiet. He stared down the length of the room at Benedict, trembling slightly, either from rage or from the fear of what lay ahead. Had he spent the night lying awake, listening to the hours tick by as the inevitable had got closer, expecting a confession, or perhaps an apology?

'These things are much harder to stop than they are to start,' Comstock said, reading his thoughts. 'And it appears that Lady Elmstead has already decided the outcome.' He cast a quick glance in her direction. 'I am sure it is not the most encouraging thing to see one's wife wearing black on a morning like this.'

'Wishful thinking,' Benedict muttered. 'Even if he beats me, he will gain nothing by this. She is not likely to be shamed and shouted into fidelity, nor will she love him any better for expressing his doubts about her to a houseful of people.'

'Let us hope that the scandal attached to this morning teaches him to keep his suspicions to himself.' Comstock consulted his watch. 'It is almost time to begin. I must ask you, one last time, if there is any way, short of violence, to settle this matter.'

Benedict shook his head. 'Let us get it over with.'

Comstock walked the length of the ballroom to confer with the other second. When it was clear he had no offer of apology to convey, they went to the footmen and began to check the weapons, testing blades and balance to make sure that the combatants had equal chance, beyond their skill.

As he waited, Benedict stared at the waiting crowd, searching for the one face he did not see. Lenore was there at Lady Elmstead's side, but it was impossible to decide if she was playing the role of worried mistress or simply taking one of the few opportunities available to comfort her lover when no one would be the wiser for it.

But there was no sign of Abigail Prescott. He could not decide if this pleased or disappointed him. On one hand, he did not want her to be a witness to violence. On the other, if there was even the smallest chance that he might die, he wished that she was there to look upon him as he passed.

He wondered if it would be too dramatic to request that she be brought to his side, should the worst occur. Then he decided against it. If the goal was to protect her, he could not demand that she weep over his bleeding body. The appropriate thing to do would have been to put his feelings for her into a letter which could be delivered in the event of his death or burned if he survived. But last night, he had been feeling much more confident about his chances and had not even considered it.

Comstock was returning with a sabre and he took it, running through the parries mechanically, prime to octave and back. Then he experimented with a lunge, advancing and retreating down the length of the ballroom to loosen his muscles.

The crowd had grown quiet. He lowered his point and walked down the row of them, staring into each face in turn. They had thought themselves bored enough to want bloodshed and eager to see a great man stumble. But now that the moment had arrived, they flinched from his gaze and looked away, ashamed.

Then the long case clock in the hall was striking six and Comstock was approaching to walk him forward to meet his opponent. Suddenly, there was a rustling in the crowd. People whispered and nudged each other, and heads turned from him as if they had just discovered something far more interesting than life or death. Then, a voice above them cried, 'Wait!'

Benedict turned to see Abby, staring down at them from the musician's gallery. Unlike Lady Elmstead's sombre black gown, she was wearing her scarlet dinner dress. Her black hair was long and loose as it had been when he'd bedded her. Arriving as she had, on the last stroke of six, Sarah Siddons could not have made a more dramatic entrance, nor better captivated the crowd.

Even from the length of half a ballroom, he could see evidence of the troubles she had described to them in his bedroom. She was paler than she had been when they'd last spoken. Her features were pinched, her brow furrowed from the pain in her head. And he saw her tremble under the gaze of the party, before she gathered strength and courage to speak again.

'There has been a horrible misunderstanding,' she announced, to the spellbound people below her. 'Lord Elmstead, if you distrust your wife because of a misplaced handkerchief, know that she did not receive it from the Duke of Danforth. She got it from me.'

There was an appropriate gasp from the audience.

She continued. 'I must have loaned it to her by mistake, for I let her borrow one just the other day.'

It was a lie. She should not have to lie for him. But

she was too far away for him to run to her and cover her mouth before she revealed the truth.

'And how did you come to have Danforth's linen?' Elmstead demanded, staring up at her, some of his bluster returning.

'Miss Prescott...' Benedict said in a warning tone, willing her to be quiet.

There was no way to stop her now. He had first been drawn to her for what he had thought was fearlessness. Though she had sworn that such courage did not exist, she was demonstrating it on his behalf. She took a dramatic pause, waiting until the nerves of the people below had stretched almost to the breaking point. Then she announced, 'I have it because I was with him two nights ago.'

The room gasped, then leaned forward, fascinated.

'I beg your pardon?' This shocked exclamation came from her own mother, who was probably hoping that she was not about to hear her daughter making the family even more notorious than it already was.

'We have been spending much time together since I arrived,' Abby hurried on. 'Every spare minute. I was with him until dawn on the night in question. He could not tell you because he did not wish to dishonour me. I took his handkerchief as a token. And then, foolishly, I lost it.'

Lady Elmstead gave a sigh of relief and dropped to the floor in a swoon. But her reaction was largely unnoticed except by Lady Comstock who produced a hartshorn from her pocket and went to revive her.

'Miss Prescott, I do not need you telling tales to

protect me,' Benedict called up to her. Years of practice had made him a master of disguising the truth. He made sure his tone implied that she was lying, though his words revealed neither truth nor falsehood.

'I am not telling tales,' she announced to the others. 'I am telling the truth. I spent the whole night in the bedroom of the Duke of Danforth and we were doing exactly what you suspect,' she repeated with more vehemence. Then, she looked to her horrified mother. 'I know it was very improper. But...' Then she gave a helpless shrug. 'And do not dare to insist that I marry him,' Abby announced, before her mother could turn her rage on the Duke. 'I refused him in London and I refused him again here.'

The room gasped.

'But you will not refuse me a third time,' he announced, making an effort to salvage what was left of her honour.

'I will indeed,' she said, turning to face him. 'You may be a duke, but you cannot force me to marry you.'

'Abigail, be reasonable,' he said. 'You have done enough.' *And now, let me do something for you.* Even if she refused him again later, an acceptance now might mitigate the scandal.

'I know what you expect from me,' she said, 'and I cannot possibly give it to you.'

The crowd leaned in again, expecting some answering confession that would reveal what more he had expected, if he'd already got her to sacrifice her virtue. But they knew far too much about his business already, without learning every last secret he shared with her. 'Abby,' he said. 'We cannot settle this here.'

'It is already settled,' she said, sadly. 'We have nothing more to say to each other.' In the silence that followed, Benedict could almost feel the eagerness of the people around them, waiting for her to exit the stage so they could discuss and dissect what they had just seen.

He turned, scanning the room for an entrance to the gallery. There should be stairs he could bound up, so he might take her in his arms and kiss her until he had changed her mind. But as with everything else in Comstock's benighted house, the staircase was not where it was supposed to be. Before he could find a way to get to her, she had obliged the crowd and made her exit, leaving only the sound of her mother's tears and the distant slam of a door.

Chapter Twenty

'It will be all right, Mama.' Abby patted her mother's hand, trying to console the inconsolable and fighting the urge to do it in time to the rise and falls of her mother's wailing. The woman had been crying since they had retreated to her room an hour ago, and the tears showed no sign of stopping. Abby had heard that it was sometimes necessary to slap hysterics, to cure them. But it did not seem right to add physical violence to the mental anguish she had already inflicted.

'We are ruined, I tell you. Utterly ruined,' her mother choked out, between sobs. 'It is one thing for people to assume that you are dishonoured, and quite another for you to…'

Announce in a crowded room that I am a strumpet?

It was kind of her mother not to finish the accusation, even if it was because she could not speak around a fresh flood of tears. Abby released her and went to the cupboard in the corner to fetch a dry handkerchief from the pile of linen that the maid had not finished packing. The roads were still muddy, but since the rain had stopped, they had decided to take their chances, rather than spending another day as objects of curiosity for Lady Comstock's guests.

Surprisingly, it mattered very little to her what they did. She had heard that confession was good for the soul and apparently it was true. Once one had announced the darkest, most ruinous secret of one's life to a crowd of talebearing strangers, one had nothing left to fear from the sort of ordinary gossip that had frightened her a day ago.

'I cannot wait to get away from here,' her mother said, taking the cloth with an accusatory sniff. 'But it will have to be back to Somerset. I can never show my face in London again. If your father were here...'

Things would be even worse, she was sure. 'He is not,' Abby said so bluntly that her mother paused in her crying. 'Nor will he be, until his money runs out and his mistress tires of his moods.'

'Abigail, you are not—'

'Supposed to speak of such things?' she finished. 'I think it is time we did, Mother. The chances are good that we will have only each other for company for a very long time. I fail to see how hoping for Father's return will make things any better for either of us.'

'But what choice do we have?' her mother demanded. 'A woman without a man is nothing in this society.'

'Then we shall have to create a new society, just for ourselves. Perhaps Lady Beverly will join us, for she seems to have little use for men.' She bit her tongue, for she had not intended to reveal secrets.

Fortunately, her mother remained oblivious. 'She will have Danforth, again, now that you have so publicly left the field of battle.'

'She has no intention of marrying him,' Abby said, easing the subject away from the truth. 'It is proof that survival without men is possible.'

'But you have no intention of becoming a kept woman,' her mother said. Then her tears stopped. 'You don't, do you?'

'No, Mama,' she said. Because of Benedict, she had the necessary knowledge, but no inclination to do such a thing with any other man in the world.

'That is some comfort,' her mother said, sighing. 'It is possible, when one is in love, to make a foolish mistake. But one should not make a habit of it.'

It was forgiveness, after a fashion, and Abby accepted it. 'If there is any chance that I might still find a husband, I will insist that you come to my house, and stay as long as you want.'

'That would be nice,' her mother said. Her tone was wistful, but compared to everything else she had said, it sounded practically rebellious. 'I don't suppose, now that you have spurned him so publicly, the Duke will offer to do right by you.'

Abby sat down beside her and patted her hand again. 'I do not think so, Mama.' He had been willing to forgive one ruined offer and had seemed ready to forgive the second one, after her confession. But even patient men learned not to bother after being turned down a third time.

'Then you should not have spoken,' her mother said.

'If you did not get a husband out of it, it did you no good at all.'

'It prevented him from duelling with someone to protect me,' she replied, feeling her throat tighten in fear of what might have happened. 'I could not bear it if he had been hurt on my account or hurt someone else and been forced to flee to the Continent.' She swallowed back a sob of her own. 'Frankly, Mama, I cannot imagine it is worth living in a country that did not have him in it.'

Now, it was her mother's turn to comfort. 'Do you love him so very much, then?'

Abby pulled out the spare handkerchief she had hidden up her own sleeve, balled it in her fist and then pressed it to her own face. Her affirmative answer came out in a wet gulp.

Now, her mother's arms were around her. 'My dear, I am so sorry. If we are able to find another man to have you, you must not make that mistake again. It is easier to be married when one does not love. One can put up with a surprising amount of difficulty when the heart is not engaged.'

If anything, this advice made her want to cry even harder. 'Oh, Mama, I am so sorry.' She had always assumed that, at some point, there had been genuine affection between her parents. But it appeared that their marriage had been empty from the beginning. 'Now that I have felt what it is like, I cannot imagine living the rest of my life with a man I do not love.'

Her mother shook her head. 'I knew it was dangerous, matching someone like you with a man like

Danforth. You are an idealist, my dear. And he is far too easy to love.'

'But I did not,' she insisted. 'Not until coming here.'

'If you'd had no feelings for him, you would have gone willingly to the altar when you had the chance,' her mother said, with a sad smile.

'I could not have loved him,' she insisted. 'How could I? We barely knew each other.'

'You loved what you wanted him to be,' her mother replied. 'And you left him when he disappointed you.'

Then she had come to know him and found that he was just what she'd hoped: faithful, honourable, dependable and kind. His only flaw was that he was so far above the problems she faced that he could not be made to understand them. So, she had left him again.

'I disappointed him as well,' she said, hoping that he was not as bothered by the break as she was. 'He wanted someone stronger than I could ever be.'

'In the end, darling, we can be only what we are, flawed and all too human.' Then, she smiled and patted her daughter's hand, just as Abby had done for her. 'We will manage somehow, I expect.'

Abby nodded, not really believing.

'We will go on as we have been. Your father will come home. He always does. It shall be just the three of us again. He will find out what has happened here eventually, of course. But I will see to it that we do not discuss the matter, if you do not wish to.' Which probably meant that her mother would take the brunt of the ranting and raving.

Abby had been hoping that her mother might be

strong enough to escape on her own and all the while her mother had been looking to her for rescue. She had been waiting for that happy moment when she might live in the shadow of a better marriage made by her daughter. But now, because of what she had done, home would be even worse. 'I have failed you,' she said.

Her mother stared at her with the most tender of smiles. 'You never could, my love. You are the best and brightest part of my life.'

Suddenly, there was a knock at the door. Before she could stand to open it, the Earl of Comstock poked his head into the room and grinned at them. 'Begging your pardons, ladies, but I strongly urge you to come to the main floor. There is an incident occurring that I think you will enjoy.'

'I am sorry, my lord. But my daughter is in distress and I cannot possibly think of parlour games at a time like this,' her mother said in a tone that was firm and, for a change, surprisingly maternal. Then she walked to the linen press and got Abby a fresh handkerchief.

Comstock laughed. 'Distress? If it pertains to Danforth, then we have just the thing to cure what ails you.' He stood in the doorway for a moment, tapping his foot, as he waited for them to relent. Then he glanced over his shoulder, as if considering what he might miss if he dallied. At last, he looked back at them with a shrug. 'Suit yourself. But you are expected to play a part in the unfolding drama downstairs. If you do not hurry, you will miss your cue.' Then he hurried away, leaving the door open behind him.

'What in heaven's name was he talking about?' her

mother said, absently, getting up to close the bedroom
door. But once on the threshold, she stopped, still and
listening. Abby watched as her ears seemed to prick
to the sound of distant voices, carrying from the hall
below. Almost without thinking, she stepped into the
hall to hear them better, instantly absorbed.

Unable to help herself, Abby rose from the bed and
followed her. Once there, it was impossible to ignore
the sound of the argument taking place in the main hall
below them. At first, she thought that the Elmsteads
were at it again. But the female half of the pair shouting on the main floor was far too vocal to be that lady
and the man sounded far too familiar.

Heads were poking from bedroom doorways and
a growing group of people was making its way to the
main stairs, trying to pretend that they just happened
to be heading down to tea and were accidentally about
to interrupt the first public argument between Danforth
and his mistress in the history of their long-standing
relationship.

Before she had even reached the head of the stairs,
Abby could hear the Duke announce, 'Do not think I
will stand here and allow you to besmirch the honour
of a young lady.'

This was answered first by a crash of breaking
china and the cry, 'Young? Is that what you want?'

Comstock, who was standing at her side, whispered,
'Lady Beverly is working her way through the curio
cabinet in the main hall.'

'Put that down that vase, you harridan, and listen
to reason.'

There was a second crash as another Comstock heirloom was lost to posterity. As they started down the stairs together, Lord Comstock said in another aside, 'Do not worry yourself about the china. We have plenty of it. Charity has told them which of the items are fair game.'

Her host was acting as if there was nothing unusual in what was happening below and had been eager for her to witness it. But was it really all for show?

'Is it unreasonable to expect fidelity?' Lenore's shriek was followed by a woof of expended rage and a china shepherdess sailed across their field of vision.

'Ah ha!' There was a masculine cry of triumph instead of a crash, which led her to believe that the Duke had caught the thing before it could break. But the quick arrival of a second projectile resulted in a cry of pain as it struck him, followed by first one crash and then a second as he dropped the figurine that he had caught. 'Blast it, Lenore. I made no promises to you. You knew I was in love with her months ago. If it weren't for your meddling, we'd have been married by now.'

There was a gasp of surprise from half the house at this juicy titbit, making Abby wonder what the other guests would say if they knew it had surprised her as well. The gist of the statement was true, she supposed. She would have married him, had it not been for his friendship with Lady Beverly. But that he loved her…?

Then she reminded herself that the Duke of Danforth did not lie.

'But I didn't know you meant to abandon me.' This

was followed by a roar of rage and the large oriental vase by the door went rolling across the entrance hall floor.

'That is Ming Dynasty,' the Countess announced in a bland voice as it crashed against the opposite wall.

'A cheap imitation,' Lord Comstock muttered, pushing Abby ahead of him to hurry her down the stairs. 'We buy replacements by the case lot. They are dead handy for holding umbrellas, but someone is always bumping into them.'

'You thought I would hold my wife and Duchess up to derision for the sake of our friendship?' Benedict stepped into view at the foot of the stairs, declaiming his lines with all the drama of Edmund Kean at the Drury Lane Theatre. 'She was to be the mother of my children, Lenore. She would always hold the first place in my heart.'

Comstock was right. Whether the story performed was true or false, this was Abby's cue to come down the stairs and play her part. Since Benedict was looking up at her with the devoted gaze of a penitent at the foot of an idol it was far too late to run back to her room and pretend that she had not seen him. She walked slowly down the stairs, still unsure what might happen when she arrived at the bottom. She assumed that they would give her some hint as to what was expected, for the whole thing seemed to be carefully scripted. Since she doubted that it would end with her being set upon, tooth and claw, by Danforth's mistress, there was no reason she could not improvise a few lines and get it over with.

Because of the Duke of Danforth and Lady Beverly, every eye in the room was on her now, just as she had always feared they would be. Every ear tuned to hear what she would say to them. All minds wondered what she was thinking. She waited for the beginnings of the terror the situation should bring.

But Benedict was looking at her as well. His expression was calm, his smile steady and one hand reached out to her in encouragement. She focused on that hand, a lifeline to cling to in a choppy sea, and walked down the stairs towards it.

Though relegated to the background, Lenore was not quite ready to give up the starring role. She threw her hand across her eyes in a gesture worthy of melodrama. 'Leave me, then. Abandon me to my shame.'

'I am not abandoning you to anything,' Benedict said, not bothering to look in her direction, clearly unmoved. 'You are beautiful. I am not the only man in England who has noticed the fact. I doubt you will be alone for long. But I will not continue to associate with someone who thinks she can be more important than the woman I love.' He was still staring up at her, watching her approach, his hand still outstretched. It was a pose worthy of an apologetic lover. Then his voice grew so quiet that only she could hear. 'How could I ever betray a woman who would put her own reputation at risk out of needless fear for mine?'

'I could not see you hurt,' she whispered back. She had forgotten that she was expected to perform for the group. It was as if she could feel the whole house straining forward, trying to catch her words.

'And I told you it would be all right,' Benedict said in reply, then gave her an encouraging smile. 'I would never, in a million years, have done what we did outside the sanctity of marriage if I thought you would be hurt by it.' He looked directly into her eyes as he spoke, his green eyes soft with apology. He'd made no effort to play to the crowd, but someone must have heard him for there were whispers and an audible sigh of admiration.

'I know,' she mouthed.

'And I will not allow you to be hurt, now,' he said. Then, he dropped to one knee as she walked down the last stairs to him and raised his voice. 'Please, Miss Prescott, I apologise for the dishonour I have brought on you. I want nothing more than to put it right in the only way I can, by renewing my offer of marriage.' He paused, considering. 'That is not totally true.'

The guests around them gasped.

He continued. 'I do want more. Far more than to offer in apology. I want you for my wife because I can think of no one I would rather have at my side, to share my life and my future.'

She was finally near enough so she could take his hand in hers and he bowed reverently over them before touching his lips to them. Then, he added, 'Abigail, my heart, I am yours for ever, regardless of your answer. I love you. Will you have me?'

Then, his lips barely moved as he whispered against her skin, 'I know you hate to be the centre of attention. But I thought a public display of my true feelings might be reassuring.' The flat tone of the Duke of Danforth had returned, just for a moment, offering a didactic explanation and making her wonder if his proposal had been sincere.

And then she remembered that Benedict did not lie. 'I do not think I mind so very much, as long as I am with you,' she whispered. Then she realised that the audience in the hall was still waiting for her answer. 'Of course, I will marry you,' she said, pulling him to his feet. He was still a step beneath her, so she was able to lean forward and kiss him tenderly on the forehead.

Apparently, that was not enough to satisfy him. He let out a whoop of joy, totally out of character with his usual, taciturn response, and wrapped his arms around her waist, lifting her feet from the step and spinning her in his arms. Then, he kissed her properly, on the mouth.

For a moment, everything and everyone around her was forgotten and she could think of nothing but the feel of his lips on hers. When he ended the kiss, she was vaguely aware of the excited chatter and well wishes of the people around her. But none of it was as important as his smile, which was broad and genuine, and seemed to light his whole face from within.

'You love me,' she said, still amazed to see it.

'I have been aware of that for quite some time,' he said. For a moment, his voice returned to the carefully modulated, emotionless tones she had grown so used to. Then the grin returned and he could not help but laugh, just a little, before saying, 'But it has been damned difficult to make you believe the fact.'

Before she could assure him that she did, he had swept her feet out from under her and tossed her over his shoulder as if she weighed nothing at all. Then, before she or anyone else could object, he was racing up the stairs with her. She was halfway to the top before she even had the sense to speak, much less resist him. 'We should not be doing this,' she said, kicking her feet ineffectually in the air. She was not sure what was about to happen, but she was absolutely certain that it was improper and that she ought to be objecting much more strenuously than she wished to.

'Pardon, ma'am,' Benedict called as they passed her mother, who was still standing, open-mouthed at the head of the stairs. Then he continued at a run until he had reached his bedroom, tossing her on to the mattress and turning to shut the door.

'We can't do this,' she said breathlessly.

'Why ever not?' he said. Now his smile was both expectant and satisfied. 'Did you not just accept my proposal? Did I not just tell everyone in the house that my romance with Lenore was at an end?'

'You had no romance with Lenore,' she said, impatient. 'And I did not actually hear you use that word, when you were arguing with her.

'Because I never lie,' he said.

'You never claimed to love her,' she said, thoughtfully. 'But you made it clear to everyone that things had changed between you. And you did say many wonderful things about me.'

'All true,' he confirmed. 'You said the other night that you would not have me if people thought I was bedding someone else.' He offered her a courtly bow. 'I trust I have made it clear to the rest of the party where my heart and future lies,' he replied, walking slowly towards her.

'Then, perhaps I shall publicly forgive her for what has already occurred between you,' she said.

'You would do that?' He gave her a smile of almost childlike delight.

She could not help but smile back. Each new tone and new expression was like a gift, another window opening on a man who had been a tightly closed mystery for years. 'We will see how able you are to withstand the gossip when your wife and former mistress are thick as thieves and telling tales about you.'

'She is a bad influence on you,' he said, smiling.

'But she has been very kind to Mother. I think it would be good for Mama to spend more time with a woman who values her independence as much as your friend Lenore.'

'An interesting plan,' he said, the corners of his lips quirking in a way that made her want to kiss him. 'For all her peculiar habits, Lenore has a very good heart.'

'Because of that, I see no reason that you can't resume your friendship with her,' she said, then added, 'After she is through mourning your lost love, of course.'

'After the wedding, at least,' he said, pocketing the key to his room door and loosening his cravat. 'I am not going to let you refuse me again, you know.'

'And when will that be?' she said. He was advancing on her with a deliberate pace and a look in his eye that would have made her knees go weak, had she been standing. 'I do not want to hear any promises about finding a vicar only to have you change your mind once you are done with me.'

'I will never be done with you,' he said, dropping his neckcloth and pulling off his coat. 'And I will have to marry you tomorrow, since the whole house knows where we have gone.'

'I suspect my mother is weeping once again for the loss of my reputation.'

'Tears of happiness,' he assured her, starting to unbutton his waistcoat. 'And I am sure it would ease her mind to see this.' He reached into his coat pocket and pulled a piece of paper from the breast pocket. Then, he unfolded it and handed it to her.

'Our marriage licence?' she said, not just surprised, but shocked. 'Why on earth do you have that here?'

For the first time since she'd met him, the formerly brooding Duke of Danforth looked sheepish. 'It was in my pocket on the day of our wedding and I have not been able to bring myself to throw it away.'

'But it has been three months,' she said, amazed.

'Almost three months,' he corrected. 'Eighty-nine days, to be precise. We have one more day left to use it. I am sure there is a vicar in the village who would be happy to perform the ceremony.'

'The roads are still very bad,' she reminded him.

'I will carry him back on my shoulders, if necessary,' he said, sitting on the bed next to her and pushing her back into the pillows. 'After this afternoon, I will have several more reasons to rescue your tattered reputation.'

'Several?' she said as he plucked at the drawstring of her bodice.

'Several,' he said, though his voice was muffled against the skin of her shoulder.

'In broad daylight,' she said, suddenly embarrassed. Then his mouth moved lower and a flash of pleasure made her forget to object.

'Everyone knows what we are doing,' he whispered. 'Just as they knew when I was with Lenore. They know all manner of things, some of which might even be accurate. But I intend to make sure that when they talk about us, there will always be something wonderfully shocking to speculate on.'

He kissed her and, for the first time in her life, she could not imagine anything nicer than the sort of scandal he was describing. 'Then let them talk,' she said as they fell back on to the bed together.

Chapter Twenty-One

Abby woke the next morning to find that her lover had gone.

For a moment, the utter trust she had placed in him on the previous afternoon was shaken to the core. The thought that she was the subject of talk had been much easier to accept when he had been only inches from her, smiling into her eyes and laughing about it. But now she was alone, wrapped in his bedsheets and unable to summon a maid to help her to her room. She could not risk the bell pull for it was unlikely to bring anyone but the valet and he would be no help at all.

There was a knock on the door, followed by a rattling of the knob.

She dived under the covers until only her eyes were visible and waited.

When the door opened, Lady Comstock appeared, followed by a maid, two footmen bearing a bathtub and her mother. Of the four of them, only the Countess seemed to be treating the matter as just another day. 'Good morning,' she said, pulling back bed and window curtains to let in the light. 'Danforth said we were to allow you to sleep. But it is already half past seven and men know nothing about the necessary preparations for a day like this.'

'What sort of day?' she said cautiously as her mother helped her into a dressing gown, shielding her from the men filling the bathtub.

'Danforth said you were to be married today.' The Countess checked the watch that was pinned to her bodice. 'And if he means to be done before the licence expires at noon, he is late in returning.'

'The roads are barely passable,' Abby said, hopping out of bed and going to the window. 'He did not have to...'

'Yes, he did,' her mother said, all traces of waffling and whimpering gone. 'I will ring for your breakfast, as you take your bath. The Countess has found a fresh muslin for you and a veil as well. You will have to make do with a bouquet of whatever garden flowers that the storm has spared.'

'I do not need a bouquet,' she said. She was tired and confused and not even sure she needed breakfast, much less another wedding that had been organised without her input.

'You will accept it and be grateful,' her mother said with a firm smile. 'You may think me a foolish old woman, Abigail, but there has been far too much nonsense between you and the Duke. It must be put right immediately before your father reappears and your husband-to-be lands in another duel.'

'Yes, Mama,' she said, still dazed and surprised at how quickly things were moving.

In a scant two hours, she had been fed, bathed and dressed, handed a nosegay of tiny pink roses and led down the stairs and through the ballroom to the chapel. The same crowd that had gathered yesterday to see men stab each other were seated in several rows of gilt-legged chairs, waiting for the festivities to start. The Comstock's daughter, Mercy, barely old enough to walk without the help of her nurse, was wandering through it all with a basket of rose petals, alternately strewing the ground and putting them in her mouth.

The only thing missing was the groom.

The Countess checked her watch again and raised an eyebrow, then led Abby to a bench in the chapel to wait.

It was past ten when the Earl appeared in the doorway to the entrance hall, gesturing to his wife, who went to speak to him. Then, he disappeared up the main stairs and the Countess returned to sit beside her.

'There have been complications,' she said, offering the Prescotts an inscrutable smile.

'The weather,' Abby said, thinking of the roads.

'Among other things,' the Countess, replied. 'Mercy, do not bother the puppy.' She disappeared for a moment to rescue the black-and-white dog who was being pelted with flower petals.

The Earl reappeared in what must have been a quick change of clothes and freshly polished boots.

'Miss Prescott. Mrs Prescott.' He bowed to each of them before setting the church register he'd been carrying at the side of the altar.

It was now ten past eleven and the guests were growing restless, as was the bride. Abby had a horrible image of her beloved, standing three months ago alone at the altar of St George's, waiting for a woman who would never arrive. Perhaps this was some horrible joke to pay her back for what she had done. Perhaps she was still asleep and it was a nightmare.

'He is not coming,' she said, staring at the Earl in resignation.

'Nonsense,' the Earl said, in a tone that was not particularly convincing. 'There were complications.'

'What complications?' She sounded shrill and far too loud. And, as they had been doing since the moment she'd arrived here, the other guests were whispering to each other, trying to imagine what was happening.

On the other side of the ballroom, the Countess was conferring with Lady Beverly, who burst into inappropriate laughter before covering her mouth and rushing from the room.

Next to her, the Earl smiled. 'There are certain conditions attached to the licence that need to be met so the marriage can be legal. You are within the three-month period—' he checked his watch '—for another thirty minutes, at least. It is not yet noon.'

'But I need a groom,' she reminded him, thinking back to the time just a day or two ago where a situation like this might have frightened her into a megrim.

She was far past headaches now, in a place where normal emotions no longer applied. 'Where is Benedict?'

'Apparently, it was also important that one of you be from the local parish,' Comstock said, gently.

'But we are from Somerset,' she replied.

'And the Danforth property is in the north,' he agreed. 'And, as of this morning, here.'

'Here?'

'I sold him a cottage in the village. Not the land, of course, since that is not mine to give. But he owns a cottage. Then we had to persuade the vicar, who wanted him to be a proper member of the parish. After some discussion of ecclesiastical law, I persuaded him that a second baptism was not necessary, but there was the matter of a mass...'

'He went to church without me?' she said, baffled.

'We can but hope so,' the Earl replied. 'I am not absolutely sure that Danforth's temper was going to hold until communion. I left during the sermon, which was rather long. The topic was fornication.'

'Oh.' She wanted to argue that there would not be a problem, for Danforth did not have a temper.

But Benedict did.

Then, the front door opened with a force that slammed it against the wall. Everyone turned to see the Duke, her Duke, her beloved Benedict, spitting fire and muddy to the waist and dragging a black-coated man through the entryway. He pushed the vicar ahead of him, towards the Comstocks, and paused, bracing himself against one footman as the other one yanked the muddy boots from his feet.

Then he stomped through the ballroom to the chapel, giving the vicar a dark look that had the man reaching to his Bible for protection. But as he arrived at Abby's side and looked down into her eyes, his anger seemed to evaporate. 'Beautiful,' he murmured. 'Just as I always imagined you would be.'

'And you…' she said, staring at him and smiling. He was stocking footed, in mud-soaked breeches and had left his dignity somewhere on the road between the village of Comstockton and the Manor's front door. He was nothing at all like the man she had seen in Almack's three months ago. But he had moved heaven and earth to be with her and arrived with fifteen minutes to spare. 'You, Your Grace, are too wonderful for words.'

* * * * *

*If you enjoyed this story check out these
other great reads by Christine Merrill*

The Wedding Game
A Convenient Bride for the Soldier

*And be sure to read the books in her
latest miniseries Those Scandalous Stricklands*

'Her Christmas Temptation'
in Regency Christmas Wishes
A Kiss Away from Scandal
How Not to Marry an Earl